TIME WARRIORS
PART ONE

Written By: Tom Tancin
Cowritten By: Chris Wolf

This series is dedicated to the many people that helped us over the years. There are so many that it is impossible to list them on this dedication page. Although this book may have been written by two people, many more were involved in the process. They know who they are, because we made sure of it.

-To Ann, you mean more to us and this series than you realize. I wish there was a way to show you that. Thank you for your support, it is greatly appreciated.

Part One (**)
The Experiment
The Secret of Atlantis
The Master of Time

Part Two
The Armies of The Zodiac
The Return to Paradise
The Elements

Part Three
Ancient Egypt
Discovery
Realization

Part Four
Quest
Destination
Forces of Time

From the Authors

This book is part of a series of four books. Each book in the series contains three missions of the Time Warriors. The books were written over the course of about eight years. We would like to take this opportunity to give you a little history on what you are about to read in hopes that you will appreciate it more.

This project is very important to us. It all started as a challenge by our seventh grade English teacher. Over the years, it turned into a prize possession. The series became an escape from adolescence. Life is rough, but if you can find something to get you through, then that 'something' is special. This series did that and that is why it is very special to us. This series bonded us as friends and tied us to many other people who helped us along the way.

Originally, we felt that we would never publish the series. We thought that it was just our escape and our hobby. In fact, most of our own friends and families were not aware of the series. However, during the closing of the series, we realized that there was more to our writing than we had thought. We realized that there were messages hidden in the team and we wanted to share them with the world. We sent the manuscript to various publishers. We were accepted a few times and rejected a few times. We had various opportunities to publish with publishing companies but we did not like what they were offering. That is why we decided to self publish. We can control what makes it to the public. You can be assured that what you read is what we wrote and that is the way it should be because we are the authors. We spent many years creating this series and it means too much to us to let it go to the public in any form other than what we wrote.

This series is a symbol of friendship and the struggles that life can put on those friendships. We are both extremely proud of this series and extremely honored to share it with you. We are extremely grateful to the people that guided us along the way. There were a few people in the beginning but there are a lot more involved today. Two high school students, who knew nothing about writing, could not have completed this series, and published it ourselves, without help. High school can be a tough experience, but when you have friends and guidance, you can make it through. We thank everyone for their continued love and support. We thank you, the readers, for choosing to let us share our journey with you. You can be assured there is a lot more to come. This is only the beginning.

Sincerely,

Tom Tancin

Chris Wolf

MISSION ONE:

THE EXPERIMENT

CHAPTER ONE

It was June of our senior year that began the very journey that I am about to explain. This is the first time that I am going to talk about it and the first time that the entire world will have a chance to read it. This is the chance for everyone to discover the truth. Time travel has always plagued the minds of humans, that is until it became a reality. What begins now, is the extraordinary adventures of the mighty warriors. They became known as the Time Warriors; and I had the honor to be the leader of the team.

What begins now, is a journal of the greatest adventures that the team faced in the first seven years of their existence. And it begins at the beginning. It all started in the hallways of our high school. It was June of our senior year, and the rest is history.

I fought my way to my locker through the crowded hallways. I pushed my way to my locker and opened it. I put my books in my locker and closed it. It was the start of the school day and I was awaiting the arrival of my friends. There was Chris, who was average build but very aggressive. He had short, black hair. My cousin Krissy, had black hair, but wasn't the average girl. She was very athletic, and was built like an athlete. Her and Chris never got along, and they always made fun of each other. Chris would tease Krissy about her size, and Krissy would snap back at him. Finally, there was my girlfriend, Heather. Heather was a typical high school girl. She was very petite and had all the girly characteristics. She had brown hair, to her shoulders. By our senior year, we had been dating for two years.

"This is going to be such a long day," Chris said as he met me in the hallway. He was paging through his history book. "I have so many tests."

"I have an English test," I replied. "And I studied all night long." I was very studious and always tried my best. Chris wasn't always that way, although he was really smart. He could do great on a test, if he only applied himself. However, like most high school students, he had his mind elsewhere. Heather also was very studious and we tried to convince Chris to try, but it never worked. Heather met us at my locker and gave me a kiss.

"How's your day going to be," Chris asked Heather. "Mine is filled with tests."

"I don't have any tests," she answered. "But don't forget, we have the speaker in physics."

"What speaker," Chris asked.

"The one on time traveling," Heather responded. "You remember don't you TJ? The one from the government that is going to explain time traveling. You know, because the government just built a time machine."

"I didn't know we were having a speaker," Chris continued with his confusion.

"He told us yesterday," I supported Heather. "How could you forget?"

"I was sleeping yesterday, remember," Chris reminded us.

"Typical," Heather replied.

"Shut up," Chris snapped back.

"If you would just pay attention," Heather lectured him. "This wouldn't happen. You need to stay awake and make the most of your education. You're supposed to sleep at night!"

"Boring," Chris said as he pretended to yawn. "Why must you always lecture me?"

"I am doing it for your own good," Heather told him. "I just want to see you succeed and make the most of your life." The bell for homeroom rang and we all grabbed our books and dispersed.

"Talk to you later," I said as I gave Heather a kiss.

"Later," Chris said as he made his way down the hall through the crowd.

"Bye," Heather said as she pulled away from my grip. "I love you."

"I love you too," I replied.

After homeroom, Chris made his way to his first class. It was history and it was time for the first test of his day. Krissy was in the same history class as him and he sat down in the seat next to her. The teacher wasn't in the room yet. "Good morning," Krissy said as she saw Chris sit down. "Are you ready for another exciting day of history." She was being sarcastic, because she normally slept through history.

"What do you mean exciting day," Chris asked. "We have a test, remember?"

"We have a test," Krissy cried in shock. "How come I didn't know about it?"

"I don't know why you didn't know," Chris replied. "She told us yesterday that the test was today."

"What's it on," Krissy asked.

"The history of your brain," Chris answered sarcastically.

"I don't know anything about that."

"I can tell." Chris rubbed his face in frustration. Mrs. Matthews walked into the room and closed the door.

"Put your notes away," Mrs. Matthews said as she set her coffee on her desk.

"Here we go," Chris cried knowing that he wasn't prepared.

"Why did people have their notes out," Krissy asked in confusion.

"Cause they thought they were pretty," Chris snapped at her. "Ahhh," he cried in frustration as he slammed his face on the desk.

"I will take any last minute questions," Mrs. Matthews told them. Krissy immediately threw her hand in the air.

"Yes Krissy," Mrs. Matthews said as she prepared herself for what was about to come.

"Do I have to take the test," Krissy asked.

"Were you here yesterday," Mrs. Matthews questioned.

"Mentally or physically," Krissy replied.

11

"Certainly not mentally," Chris put his two sense in.

"Shut up," Krissy cried.

"Yes Krissy," Mrs. Matthews informed her. "You have to take the test." Mrs. Matthews handed out the tests and then sat down at her desk. Chris looked at the test and took a deep breath before starting.

Meanwhile, Heather and I were in our calculus class. We had a substitute today. The substitute didn't have anything for us to do, so we could talk quietly.

"I can't wait for physics," I told Heather.

"Me either," she replied. "I am curious to know what he is going to say about it."

"I want to know how it works," I continued. "I want to time travel; it would be so cool."

"I don't think it is a good idea for people to time travel," she commented.

"Why not? It would be a lot of fun!"

"Depends on where you go. It could be dangerous."

"They would never let you go to a dangerous place. It wouldn't be allowed."

"That makes me feel secure. How are they supposed to limit where you travel?"

"I don't know, but think of the possibilities. The possibilities are endless.

CHAPTER TWO

Third period was physics for all four of us. We all met in the classroom and sat together. In fact, we were lab partners. "This should be cool," I said.

"Yeah," Chris replied. "I'm actually going to stay awake for physics today." Heather shook her head at his comment.

"I'm not," Krissy told us. "I need my sleep and these table make for a good head rest."

"Alright," Mr. Edlin began. "I want you all to give your utmost attention to Mr. Harrison. He is an agent from the Department of Time Travel, who is here to explain the whole process. Mr. Harrison, they are all yours."

"Thank you," Mr. Harrison replied as he walked to the center of the room. "As you all know, the United States government has created a time machine and is going to test it soon. Time Travel has always plagued the minds of humans. That's why we embarked on the quest to create a time machine. The government gathered up the best scientists in our country and put them in the best lab facility we have. They paid them a lot of money and gave them the best equipment we could find. Our goal was to become the first country in the world to have a time machine. Obviously we succeeded.

The way it works is that the time machine spins so fast that it changes the atmosphere around it. It then can find the time belt, as we call it, which is the part of the atmosphere that allows us to travel in time. Once the time belt is found, the machine uses a synthetic element to punch a hole in the belt. The hole becomes a wormhole, attaching two mini black holes. One of the black holes is where the machine is, the other is the destination. The whole process has to do with the spinning velocity and the synthetic element. When everything is calculated correctly by the machine, the trip is a success. I will now take questions."

"How does the machine know where to go," a girl asked.

"Good question," Mr. Harrison replied. "The machine has time records memorized in it. We entered them in by hand so that the machine can find anytime; past, present, or future."

"How could you input the future," a boy asked. "When you don't know what the future holds."

"Another excellent question," Mr. Harrison responded. "What we did is that we taught the machine to search for a time by itself. When I said we put the records in, what I meant is that we taught the machine to search to see if the time exists."

"You said that they are going to test it," another boy asked. "Who is the 'they' you speak of?"

"Our next step is to make sure that the machine can transport humans. We sent recording instruments and it was a success, but we don't know how it reacts with humans. We want to see what kind of stress is put on the human body during the 'warping' process. As for who we are going to use to test it, we are looking at young adults your age. That is why we are talking to seniors now. We want graduating seniors to come out of high school and train with us, and then become our time traveling team."

"How would we go about getting involved," I asked.

"You would have to find a team, then sign up. After having parental consent of course. Each state will have a competition, the winning team from each of the fifty states will head to nationals. The winning team at nationals, would be the Time Warriors, as we call them."

"That would be really cool," I responded.

"I think we should do it," Chris added. "I wanna kick some ass!"

"Excuse me," Mr. Edlin yelled.

"Sorry," Chris replied.

"I think it's dangerous," Heather commented.

"It can be," Mr. Harrison told us. "But we want young adults because your bodies are at the perfect stage. You are young enough to take the extreme stress that could be witnessed. You are also energetic enough to deal with the adventure, yet you are old enough to be independent."

"Sounds like fun," Chris said.

"What are we talking about," Krissy asked.

"Go back to lala land," Chris told her.

"Already there," Krissy responded. The bell rang and the class dismissed themselves into the hallway. I went up to Mr. Harrison and waited to talk to him.

"What can I do for you," he asked.

"I want to sign up," I told him.

"Get your team together," he instructed. "Get your parents' consent, if your not eighteen and then call me. Here is my card with my number and email." He handed me the card and I looked at it. "Write your team member names down so I can tell the Pennsylvania Department of Time Travel." I did as he told me. "Someone will be in touch with you."

"Thank you," I replied and I met the other three and we left for lunch. We made our way to the cafeteria and waited in line. All four of us were over eighteen, but I still wanted my parents support.

"This will be so cool," Chris said.

"I agree," I replied.

"I don't think it is as good as it sounds," Heather commented.

"What are we doing," Krissy asked with confusion.

"We are going to take part in the biggest, most extravagant event of all time," Chris told her.

"Wow," Heather replied, "big words Chris. That's a step up."

"I know what I am talking about every so often," Chris responded as we got our food. We sat down at our normal table and prepared to eat.

"I can't eat," I said. "I'm too excited."

"I'll take it," Krissy replied already inhaling hers.

"Come up for air," Chris told her.

"I'm starving," she responded. "I didn't eat breakfast today."

"Wow, that's ten less than normal," Chris replied.

"Shut up," Krissy cried still eating.

"I'll go, for you," Heather told me. "But I'm not sure about it."

"Don't worry so much," I told her. "We will be in the government's hands. They won't let anything happen to us."

"That's what I am worried about," Heather replied.

CHAPTER THREE

"I'll see you tonight," I told Heather as we made our way out of the school

building.

"Alright," she replied. "Around seven, right?"

"Yeah," I answered. "I love you." I gave her a kiss and watched her get in her

car and drive off. I got in my car and headed home. When I got home, I went right to my

room to get my homework done. My parents weren't home yet, and I was going to ask

them at supper.

We all sat down for supper at the dining room table. My brother was already

digging into his full plate. "How was school," my dad asked us.

"Good," my brother Corey answered. He was two years younger than me with

buzzed brown hair. He could eat a lot, in fact he never stopped.

"How about you," my mom asked me.

"It was great," I replied with enthusiasm.

"What are you so excited about," my dad questioned.

"We had a speaker in physics today," I explained. "He gave an awesome speech on time traveling."

"So...," my dad replied.

"Let me finish," I told him. My parents nodded in agreement to let me go on. "He said that they are letting groups of graduating seniors volunteer to test it out. There will be state competitions and the top team from each state will go to nationals to compete. The winning team will become the Time Warriors and work for the Department of Time Travel."

"You're not thinking about going," my mom asked in fear. "Are you?"

"Well, we wanted to enter," I answered.

"Who," my dad asked.

"Chris, Krissy, Heather, and me," I replied. "So, what do you think?" My parents looked at each other. "This is the greatest opportunity of my life."

"It sounds too dangerous," my mom told me. "The words 'testing time travel' make me nervous. I don't think it is a good idea."

"Mom," I cried, "I'm going to do this. I don't need your consent because I am eighteen, but I want your support."

"You know I support you in everything you do," she replied. "But I don't agree with your decision."

"This is my one opportunity to do something out of the ordinary," I told them. I was just a regular kid that did well in school. I didn't stand out among my peers but I wanted to. This was my chance to make something of myself.

"I think it is extremely dangerous," my mom continued. "And that scares me. But if it is what you want, then I will support you."

"Thank you," I said. "That's all I wanted." The phone rang and I answered it.

"My parents are going to support me," Chris told me. "They weren't thrilled, but they will show support."

"Mine too," I replied. "I'm eating dinner; I'll talk to you later."

"Sounds good," Chris responded. I hung up the phone and returned to the table. We finished dinner while I explained how time traveling works.

Later that night I went to Heather's house. I was sitting in her computer chair facing her. She was laying on her bed; writing in her diary. "What did your parent's say," I asked.

"They will support me," she answered. "They are confident that you will protect me." I smiled at her and nodded my head.

"My parents are going to support me," I told her. "Chris' parents are ok with it also."

"This is really dangerous," Heather told me. I stood up from the chair and laid down next to her on the bed. I looked in her diary.

"What are you writing about," I asked. She closed the diary and put it to the side.

"I was writing about you," she answered.

"What about me," I questioned.

"How wonderful you are," she replied. "How much I love you and want to spend the rest of my life with you."

"You know I will never let anything happen to you," I said.

"I know," she told me. "That is why my parents are supporting me. They know how much you love me and will do anything to protect me."

"I love you so much," I said. I pushed her hair out of her face and kissed her. She rolled over and laid on her back and I put myself over top of her. I kissed her again and put my hand on her stomach. Her door opened and she pushed me off and sat up.

"We're having ice cream," Heather's mom said as she peered in. "If you two want some you are more than welcome to join us."

"We'll be down in a minute," Heather replied with anxiety that her mom would say something about catching us in that predicament.

"Leave your door open," Heather's mom said.

"Yes mom," Heather responded. Heather's mom walked down the steps and I kissed Heather.

"That was close," I told Heather. She smiled at me and kissed me again. She stood up and pulled my arm for me to follow. We headed downstairs to the kitchen. When we got to the kitchen, Heather's mom got us each a bowl of ice cream. I stood behind Heather and wrapped my arms around her while we watched her mom scoop the ice cream. We sat at the kitchen table and ate the ice cream.

"Let's go for a drive," Heather said to me.

"Can I go," Heather's little brother Jimmy asked.

"No," Heather told him.

"You're not going anywhere," Heather's mom said.

"Why not," Heather asked in confusion.

"Because it is too late," her mom continued. "You are not going with him tonight."

"But you let me all the other times," Heather said.

"I'm sorry," her mom told her. "but your dad and I want to spend time with you tonight."

"But I don't want to spend time with you," Heather screamed in anger. "I want to spend time with my boyfriend."

"Don't use that tone with me young lady," her mom replied. "You spend enough time with him. And besides you will be spending time while you are time traveling. But your father and I will not have time to spend with you."

"I'll go home," I told Heather as I got up from the table. Heather stood up and came over to me. "I'll see you tomorrow," I said.

"This isn't fair," she yelled at her mom.

"Get upstairs to your room," her mom reprimanded her.

"Fine," Heather screamed back. She gave me a hug and a kiss and stormed up to her room.

CHAPTER FOUR

The next morning at school, we were all standing by my locker. "What did your parents say," I asked Krissy.

"About what," Krissy replied.

"Did you ask," Chris responded.

"Ask what," Krissy questioned.

"Ask if they will support you if you go," I answered.

"Go where," Krissy said with confusion.

"Ahhhh," Chris screamed as he smashed his head into the locker.

"How could you forget," Heather asked.

"You know you would remember if it involved food," Chris told her.

"So what if I love food," Krissy said.

"There is more to life than food," Chris replied. "Put it this way, I eat to live. That's all I need."

"Well I live to eat," Krissy told him. "Is there a problem with that?"

"I give up," Heather cried.

"I did ask," Krissy continued. "They will support me. I just wanted to get you all going."

"Very funny," Heather cried. "You always have to frustrate us."

"Yes," Krissy told her. "Because it's fun."

"I will call Mr. Harrison tonight," I told them. "Then I will let you know what he says."

"Sounds good," Chris replied.

"I'm sorry about last night," Heather told me quietly as she came over and wrapped her arms around me. She laid her head on my chest.

"It's fine," I told her. "I understand that your parents wanted to spend time with you."

"But I wanted to be with you," she said. The bell rang and the halls started to clear. We all headed for the gym for graduation practice. We were done with classes because it was our last week. Graduation was just a few days away and we were getting nervous. Once graduation happened, we began our emergence into the real world. Graduation was special. All our families were there. Heather and I had a graduation party together. It was a chance for my whole family to meet Heather's whole family. Soon, graduation was behind us and we were ready to face the world and try to become the Time Warriors.

Over the next few weeks, we trained every day. We ran two miles, twice a day. Then we headed to the gym and worked with equipment. By the end of July, we were required to be in Harrisburg to prepare for the Pennsylvania state competition. Obviously, since I am telling you the story, we won the state and national competitions. The state competition involved mental and physical tests. We were required to answer science, math, and history questions as a team for the mental part. Physical tests included obstacle courses, races, swimming, and rock climbing. We were crowned Team Pennsylvania and were sent to Washington D.C. for the national competition.

There were teams from every state in the country. The national competition was much harder. It contained various tests that eliminated teams at each level. It came down to us, Team Pennsylvania, and Team Missouri. Team Missouri contained Danny, Megan, Eric, and Erica. We didn't like Team Missouri from day one because they were obnoxious. Needless to say, we beat Team Missouri and they weren't happy about it. However, Team Missouri wouldn't disappear out of our lives anytime soon. You'll see what I'm talking about.

We met Dr. Johnson during the national competitions. He was the leading time travel scientist. Johnson would become the most important man in our lives in a matter of days. He was short and chubby and always dressed in a white lab coat.

The day to leave finally came and we were in the lobby of the FBI building. The Department of Time Travel worked out of the FBI building. The media was everywhere and all of our parents were there. Johnson walked over and shook our hands. "TJ is the leader," Johnson told the others. "You need to listen to everything he tells you. Heather, you are second in command. If anyone should challenge him, it's Heather." She smiled at me. "You have five days in time to explore what you wish. In those five days you will be able to tell if it works or not. If you are not back in five days, the other team, Team Missouri, will be sent to rescue you."

"You won't need that," I said. "If the situation is that bad, Danny certainly won't be able to save us." Danny gave me an evil look.

"Ok," Johnson said, "let's do this." He led us down the hallway but he wouldn't let us say goodbye to our parents. The media cameras followed us down the hallway taking pictures and yelling questions. He led us into a stairwell and then we walked down the steps. The reporters were not allowed to follow us once we got to the stairwell. It was silent while he led us. We were getting ready to embark on the most dangerous journey ever. When we got into a large room he turned around to face us.

"There on the wall," he said as he pointed to the wall. "Those are your outfits." They were black jeans, black boots, a belt, and a white T-shirt that said "Time Warriors" on the pocket. We ran over and got dressed quickly, then he led us out of the room.

"Alright," he said. "You're ready."

"So where's the time machine," Chris asked.

"Right here," he answered. He pulled the fabric off a huge contraption. We stood in awe. He pressed the button on the door and it opened. We walked in and sat down. We were prepped numerous times on how to control the machine. "Good luck and God bless, Warriors," he said as the door closed. I pressed the button and the machine started to shake.

"Oh my God," Heather screamed. "What's going on?"

"It's ok," I replied. "It's just getting started." The shaking got worse.

"What if it explodes," Krissy asked.

"What," Heather asked Krissy. "It's going to explode?"

"No," I answered. "It won't explode." The machine started to spin and the stress on our bodies was increasing. Johnson stepped back and watched as it spun.

"It hurts," Heather screamed.

"Hold on," I told her as I grabbed her hand.

"Did you put the time period in," Chris asked.

"Oh shit," I replied. "I didn't."

"Put it in now," Krissy added. I punched in 1900, just so I got a year in the computer.

"Not accessible," the machine spurted out at me.

"What," I said in shock. "How can that be?"

"Maybe it doesn't work," Krissy said. "It might be busted."

"Your face is going to be busted if you don't shut up," Chris told her. I punched in 1776.

"Maybe it will register the revolution," I said.

"Not Accessible," the machine replied.

"Come on," I yelled at it. Johnson stepped back some more and wondered why the machine wasn't leaving.

27

"Try the future," Chris told me.

"What year," I asked.

"2020," Heather said. "That's a good show." I punched in 2020.

"Not accessible," the machine told me again.

Chris punched the wall and the machine stopped in the air.

"What did you do," Krissy asked him.

"Nothing," he replied.

"Then why did it stop," Heather asked.

"It didn't," I replied. "He hit the emergency warp button accidentally."

"So what's it going to do," Chris asked me.

"Send us to a random time," I replied. Just then Johnson felt the wind pick up and a black hole appeared under the machine.

"They're leaving," Johnson screamed with joy. The machine started to shake again. Heather almost fell over. It started to spin and went into the black hole. Suddenly it was out of sight and Johnson was dancing around. The machine was spinning really fast. There was an explosion and the machine rocked.

"We're going to die," Heather cried.

"No we're not," I calmed her. The Earth suddenly stopped with the explosion and the machine fell toward the Earth. We screamed with the feeling of falling. The breaks came on and the machine landed softly on the ground. I opened the door and stepped out very slowly. I looked around to take in the surroundings. There were no people in sight. I didn't see the revolution, or anything for that matter.

"Where are we," Heather asked.

"I don't know," I replied. "But the real question is, when are we?"

CHAPTER FIVE

The temperature seemed rather tropical. I looked for any sign that would tell us when we were. "I don't know when we are," I told the others. Then we heard something in the field behind us. We turned around and stumbled backwards in amazement. It was a field filled with dinosaurs.

"We're in the age of the reptiles," Chris told us.

"Great," Heather said. "We survive the time warping process to get eaten by a giant lizard." I looked up to the sky and saw flying reptiles. I was stunned at the sight. Not only were we the first people to time travel but we were the first people to see dinosaurs.

"I hate to kill the welcoming party," Krissy said. "But I think the time machine is broken."

"What would make you say that," Chris asked.

"Oh I don't know," Krissy continued. "The fact that there is smoke coming out of it." I walked over and looked at it. The smoke was coming from the panel with the time records.

"We blew a circuit in the time records," I told them.

"Whose we," Krissy asked. "You're the one that forgot to put the time in. Then it got overloaded when you put three time periods in."

"Chris pressed the emergency button," Heather said

"No I didn't," Chris told her. "I punched the wall and hit it accidentally."

"You can't punch these things," she told him "They are too fragile."

"Look," I said. "No matter what, we are stuck here for five days. Then the other team will come and get us. We can use their machine to get home. Until then we try to survive, it really shouldn't be that hard." Just then there was a thud and a roar.

"You just jinxed us," Heather said to me.

"What is that," Krissy asked. The trees started to move and the dinosaurs in the field ran.

"This doesn't look good," Chris said in fear. A giant dinosaur popped out from the trees.

"Don't move," I told the others. "I remember that from Jurassic Park."

"That only works for a t-rex," Heather reminded me. "This doesn't look like a rex." The dinosaur ran toward us and we made our way to the trees.

"Climb a tree," Chris yelled to us. We quickly made our way up to the top of a tree. The dinosaur continued past us and further into the woods.

"Alright," I said, "coast is clear." We climbed down and stood in a small circle.

"This is not a good situation," Chris told us. "We're stuck here for at least five days alone with these monsters."

"Wait," I said. "Do you hear that?"

"What," Heather asked.

"Water," I continued. "I hear a river." I ran through the woods until I came to the riverside. "If we build a camp near the water," I told the others when they caught up to me. "We'll be able to drink."

"Yeah," Chris said. "And the dinos will come to drink too."

"So we find a waterfall," Heather replied. "The dinos won't use a waterfall as a water source, but we can."

"Great idea," I added. We started to walk up river. Finally we got to a waterfall and there was a ledge that was perfect for setting up camp. "We need to set up tents."

"How would you suppose we do that," Krissy asked.

"Take sticks and build the structure. Use plant fibers to tie the sticks together and then cover the roof with leaves. Then put leaves on the ground for padding," I replied.

"Wow," Heather said. "You're good."

"I'm the leader," I replied. "I have to be." I walked over and grabbed some branches from a nearby tree. I took a plant that looked strong and pulled it out of the ground. Then I tied bundles of the branches together using the plant fibers as ropes. I stood them up and pushed them into the ground to make four corners. Chris followed what I was doing to make another. Krissy was having difficulty with hers. Heather was going to share mine. Then I took branches and connected them on top to make a roof. I grabbed leaves from the tree and threw them on top. Then I put some on the ground to make padding. Chris finished his too and then we helped Krissy. By the time we had finished that, the sun was setting.

"I'm hungry," Krissy said.

"Me too," Heather added.

"What can we eat," Chris asked.

"Fruit," I told them, "there might not be too many fruit trees around because they are not dominant yet, but there should be some." I ran into the woods and they stood there wondering if I was crazy. I came back with a variety of fruits and dropped them in front of them. "Dig in," I said. They started to eat but I wanted to take care of something first.

"Aren't you going to eat," Heather asked.

"It's going to be dark soon," I told her. "I need to start a fire." I grabbed some dead twigs and leaves from the ground and threw them in a pile. Then I started to rub two sticks together. I couldn't get the fire started.

"Just forget it," Chris told me. "You won't get it." I decided to listen to him and went over and sat down. The sun was below the horizon and it was getting really dark.

"This is scary," Heather said. "Those monsters are out in those woods in the dark." I picked up a piece of fruit and started to eat it.

"This is good," I said. "It's fresh."

"Don't worry," Chris told Heather. "We do what we have to do. If we get attacked, we'll worry about it then." I finished the piece of fruit and threw the core into the woods.

"Alright," I continued as I stood up. "Let's get some sleep." Krissy went into her tent and Chris into his. Heather and I went in and laid down.

"This is really cool," Heather told me.

"What is," I asked.

"The fact that you and I are alone in this tent," she continued. "We don't have our parents breathing down our necks. We can do whatever we want."

"It is cool isn't it," I replied. I kissed her and wrapped my arms around her.

In the middle of the night I was woken up by a rustling noise. Heather sat up and looked at me. I signaled for her to be quiet. I heard Krissy scream. I ran out of the tent and Heather followed me. Chris met us outside of his tent. Krissy was standing at the edge of the woods and she was surrounded by four dinos. These were smaller than the on in the field. They stood about six feet tall but were more evil looking. They had sharp claws on their arms and feet. Chris grabbed a stick from the ground.

"Hey over here," he yelled to the dinos. One made its way over to Chris. One stayed by Krissy. Two ran over to Heather and I. Chris was getting ready to hit the dino as it ran at him but I grabbed him by the arm and pulled him out of the way. The dino slid past him and into the water. The one jumped at Krissy and she ducked. The dino jumped over her and into the river. One came after me and I moved as it slid into the river. The last one jumped at Heather and she tried to avoid it but it knocked her in the river. I jumped in after her and Chris picked up a log. Chris yelled to the dino and they climbed out of the river. Heather was almost at the edge of the waterfall. I swam faster toward her. I caught her arm right before she went over. I grabbed on to a rock that was sticking out of the water. The currents were strong. Heather was slipping out of my hand and was dangling over the side of the waterfall. She screamed as she looked down. I used all my strength to pull her up and fight the currents at the same time. Chris ran down the bank and I pushed Heather toward him and he grabbed her. Then he stuck a stick out and I grabbed on and he pulled me to shore. We sat down and caught our breath.

"These dinos are different than Jurassic Park," Chris said.

"That's because it depends what era we are in," Heather responded. "We could be in any part of the dinosaur age."

"I can't identify them," I told them. "I only know the ones from Jurassic Park." When we were ready we walked back to the tents and went back to bed.

CHAPTER SIX

When we woke up the next morning, the sun was already high in the sky. I figured it was late in the morning. I crawled out of the tent and stood up. Heather joined me shortly after. We were standing on the edge of the river. "Today," she said. "And then three more days of this horrible place."

"Is it really that bad," I asked her. "I mean it is really clean and relaxing."

"But it has people-eating lizards," she continued.

"Are you sorry we took this trip," I asked.

"No," she replied. "Not totally. Yet."

Meanwhile back in Washington D.C., in the present, Mr. Harrison was in his office with Danny. "I thought you said my team would win," Danny said.

"I tried Danny," Mr. Harrison replied. "You can't say I didn't. I didn't think we would find a better team."

"But you didn't make us the warriors," Danny continued.

"I did what I could."

"Why didn't you tell them I am your son?"

"Because they wouldn't have let you go on that account anyway."

"Why?"

"Because that's the rule."

"Well it's a stupid rule."

"Look, Danny, when they don't come back in four days you will go anyway."

"Maybe they'll make it back."

"No, they won't."

"How can you be sure, dad?"

"Let's just say I played around with the time records."

"Are you serious?"

"Yeah, I made sure they got stuck in the most isolated time period ever."

"Where? How did you do that?"

"I found Johnson's plans and that showed me that I could make it so the time records didn't register with the computer."

"So what did that do?"

"It meant that when they put their time periods in, they didn't register in the computer because I already had one saved in the computer. Then the only thing for them to do would be to hit the emergency warp button. When they did that, my saved time would register, making them think that they caused it. My saved time period is the most isolated time period ever. There are no people around. They are in the time of the dinosaurs." Danny laughed evilly.

"So they won't make it back. Then we'll have to save them."

"No, wrong again. When you and your team go to save them, you won't. You'll leave for the mission, but you'll have a whole other plan on your mind. The rescue operation is supposed to be hope for them, but indeed it's only going to be their worst nightmare." They both laughed evilly. Just then Johnson walked in.

"What do you want," Danny asked him.

"I didn't do anything to you," Johnson said.

"I should get you fired," Mr. Harrison stepped in.

"Why," Johnson questioned.

"You took my son's dreams from him," the leader continued.

"I didn't take anyone's dreams," Johnson continued.

"Well," Danny butted in. "I will."

"What do you mean by that," Johnson asked. Danny pushed past him and walked down the hall. "What do you mean," Johnson screamed at Danny. Danny continued to walk down the hall and his dad followed. Johnson ran after them.

Meanwhile in paradise, Chris and I were working on the time machine. "Alright," I said. "These instructions say that we need to connect all the color wires."

"There are no wires," Chris told me. "All that's here are computer chips."

"Ok," I replied. "So maybe I'm looking at the wrong page." I flipped through the instructions. I found a page about the time records. "I got it," I told him. "The book says 'the time records are stored on computer chips. When the time is put in the computer, it registers with the computer chip."

"That's great," Chris screamed. "But how do I fix it?"

"I don't know," I responded. "But don't scream at me." Chris slammed the compartment shut and stormed off. He walked into the woods.

"Chris," Heather yelled to him. "I don't think that's a good idea." There was no response.

"You two go find him," Krissy told us. "I'll watch the camp." Heather and I walked after him. Suddenly, he stopped and looked around.

"What's he doing," Heather asked me.

"I have no idea," I replied. Just then I heard movement over to the side. I looked over there and saw two huge dinosaurs. "He's watching the stegosauruses," I told her excited that I was able to identify a species. The steggys noticed that we were there and came toward us. "Watch the tails," I told Heather and Chris. They let out a cry and then they started charging at us. One swung its tail at Chris but he ducked under it. The other swung it's tail at Heather and I but we jumped over it. Heather and I started to run and it chased us. I pushed her down just as its tail swung over us. We got back up and continued to run but another caught us from the front and swung its tail at us. We ducked under it and then jumped over the one from behind us. Chris met us and we ran from the two behind us. Chris was watching them. Heather and I saw the one come from the front.

"Chris duck," I yelled as Heather and I ducked.

"Where," Chris asked as he turned around. Just as he did the tail impacted him and he went flying backwards and hit a tree. He tumbled forward and laid on the ground trying to catch his breath. The steggys left and we Heather and I ran over to Chris.

"Are you alright," I asked with concern.

"I think so," he mumbled through the pain.

"The spikes didn't cut you did they," Heather questioned. Chris looked at his arms and then lifted his shirt. He had bruises, but no cuts.

"Let's head back to camp," I told them. "I don't like the idea that Krissy is alone."

CHAPTER SEVEN

We continued to walk through the woods but it seemed to be taking longer than it should have. I was looking around for a familiar landmark but I did not see any. Just then a small dinosaur ran across the field. He got half way out into the field and stopped in his tracks. I heard a scream from above. I looked up and saw a flying reptile swoop down and grab the dino.

"You want of piece of me," Chris screamed at the flying reptile as he threw a rock at it. The ptero, I'll call it because I don't know what species it was, avoided it but swooped down at Chris and knocked him over. It flew back up and screamed again. Another ptero joined him. Chris got up. "C'mon you piece of shit," Chris continued. The ptero swooped down at Chris and slashed his arm. Chris grabbed his arm and was really angry. The other ptero swooped down at Heather and I but we hit the ground before it could cling on to us. Then they screeched and another joined the flock. Chris picked up another rock and threw it. This time it hit one and they screeched even louder. There was a total of eight pteros circling above us.

"We have to get out of here," Heather told me. "They're going to kill us." We started to run. They swooped down and caught up to us.

"When they get closer," I told the others, "back flip onto their backs." They came closer and we slowed down. When they got right behind us we back flipped onto their backs. They rose into the air. "Lay down and hold onto their necks," I yelled to Heather and Chris. Chris didn't listen and was still standing.

"Hey guys," he yelled with adventure in his voice. "I'm ptero surfing, ha ha ha."

"Chris watch the others," I told him. "They're going to come after you." He still didn't listen and two others swooped down and knocked him down on the ptero. The wind pushed him off the ptero's back. He fell toward the ground but the ptero swooped down and grabbed a hold of him by his arms.

The ptero I was on became really annoyed with me. It went higher and flew upside down so I would be pulled down by gravity. I grabbed onto its neck harder and it swooped down close to the ground. It turned right-side up and flew up and then back down. When I knew it wasn't going to go any closer to the ground, I jumped off. I curled up and rolled as I hit the ground.

The ptero that Chris was hanging on swooped toward the ground and he loosened himself from its talons. He fell to the ground and rolled with impact. Heather screamed as she jumped off hers. I caught her and fell backwards as she landed. We ran quickly toward the woods to take cover in the trees. Once we got in the forest we brushed ourselves off. We continued to walk back to camp.

When we finally managed to find our way back to camp it was dark out. Krissy was in her tent sleeping. Chris, Heather, and I decided to sit out on the edge of the river. Heather knelt and cupped some water to splash on her face. She did that about three more times and then decided she was going to splash some water at me. I got up and went over to her. I took some water in my hands and through it at her. She screamed and started to laugh. She got up and ran toward me. I ran as she chased me around camp. Chris was laughing at us as he sat in the middle of camp.

Heather decided she had enough and so we sat down with Chris. We were talking for a little while. Chris stretched his arms out and yawned. "Come on," Heather said as she got up and pulled my arm. I stood up and she led me into the tent. Chris just smiled and then he decided to head into his tent.

The next morning we woke up and sat outside. It was day three and there were only two more days to go.

Meanwhile in the present, the media was using our story for publicity. It was in all the magazines, on the news everyday, and the headlines of the newspapers. My mom and dad were eating breakfast and reading the newspaper. It was a Saturday.

"Look at this," my mom said, "the 'Time Warriors' are said to be in need of some big 'TIME' help." She shook her head. "They shouldn't be allowed to do this. The kids had a five day deadline. It has only been three days. That doesn't mean that they need help. I don't know where they get this stuff." She got up from the kitchen table and walked into the living room. She turned the news on. "Good morning," the newscaster said. "Our top story today is the newest government team, the Time Warriors.

They are said to be lost in time. Another team is hard at work preparing to go on a rescue mission." She couldn't listen to it anymore. She pushed the play button on the VCR because she taped a late-night talk show, since they were going to talk about us.

"Just in today," the host said. "This picture." It came up on the screen and it had the four of us on it and we were standing in front of a clock. "Excuse me," the host mocked us as the audience laughed. "What time is it?" He started to laugh with the audience. Then a picture of us standing in front of a t-rex came on the screen. We had tears streaming from our eyes. "Also," he continued. "They were caught crying for their mommies and there was a t-rex saying 'I am your mommy now'". He continued to laugh. "The Time Warriors are now time wussies." He kept laughing. My mom turned the TV off and walked out of the room.

Back in paradise, we decided to take a walk to kill time. We all went this time because I wouldn't let Krissy stay at the camp by herself. We found our way to the top of a beautiful cliff with a waterfall. The waterfall was huge and it sent off mist forever. This was much more magnificent than Niagara Falls. "This is beautiful," Heather said.

"Wow," Krissy exclaimed as she stood in awe. The forest extended for miles and miles. The leaves on the trees were the greenest green I ever saw. The water falling from the waterfall was pure and clean. Then I looked across the canyon and saw gigantic dinosaurs grazing on the leaves of trees. There were flying reptiles overhead and nests of dinosaurs below on the ledges.

"This is stuff you only dream of," Heather continued as she looked around in astonishment. "You could never find a place like this in our time." We continued up the cliff until we were upstream from the waterfall. Heather put her arm around my waist.

"Maybe we should let you two alone," Chris said as he signaled Krissy to leave. They walked off into the distance toward camp and disappeared. I knew this was nice but I also knew it wasn't going to last.

CHAPTER EIGHT

Heather and I stood there admiring the view. "I wonder what is happening in our time," she said. "I wonder if they care."

"I'm sure they do," I replied. "This is a big story."

"Do you really think we will become Time Warriors?"

"I believe Johnson. I think we can trust him." The sound of Time Warriors put shivers up my spine. She held me closer and kissed me. I pushed her hair back. We continued to kiss when I felt the ground start to shake. I was concerned but she continued to kiss me. The trees started moving. I pulled away from her and turned toward the trees as the dino from the field popped out. We started running toward the woods on the side of us. The dino chased after us and it was catching up to us. I knew our only option was to jump off the cliff. My only worry, it was about eighty feet straight down to a fast moving river, then over a few waterfalls to camp. But since it was that or get eaten, I grabbed Heather's arm and pulled her toward the edge.

We screamed as we fell toward the river. When we hit the water we took a deep breath right before we went under. I held onto her arm and struggled to pull us to the surface. We gasped for air as we shot out of the water. The currents continued to take us downstream and I tried to fight them by swimming toward shore, but it didn't work. We went over a smaller waterfall and then another one. Finally we got by camp and the currents died down. We swam to shore and waited for Krissy and Chris to return.

Meanwhile back in Washington, Danny and his team were holding a meeting. "Now you know our objective is to kill them," Danny explained to his team. "And you have to be ready soon because the President has asked to move on with the rescue mission. He is worried about the media making the U.S. look bad."

"Right," Megan said. "We go to the time of the dinosaurs and kill four people with the permission of the government."

"Wrong," Danny replied. "Technically we don't have permission from the government. My dad told us to do this, not the government."

"Great," Erica butted in. "We're going to be framed."

"No we're not," Danny told her. "We need to tell the public that we found only the time machine, in pieces, and no sign of them except some body parts near the time machine."

Mr. Harrison walked in and joined the group. "You better go," he told them. "Before someone stops you." Danny and the team stood up. "Wait," Mr. Harrison said. "Take these," he threw them each a gun. "Don't come back until its done."

"You got it," Danny replied as he walked away.

CHAPTER NINE

"**I** need to address the nation," the President continued. "That is my job and they need to know the details of the whole operation."

"You can't," the Mr. Harrison informed him. "We do not have enough information and the first thing they are going to ask is if they are stranded in time. At this point, we don't know anything about the mission. We don't know if the machine even worked and where it would have taken them. However, the other team is preparing to leave, or they may have left already."

"Then that's what I will tell them," the President added. "They need to know something. The public deserves to know something."

"This should be on a tell when we have the information basis," Mr. Harrison continued. "Not just telling them something to ease their minds. When they need to know the information, then you can tell them. But you can't tell them the information they need to know until you know the information yourself and at this point you don't know that."

"Well," the President said sharply. "Then you better get me the information before I make my speech tonight at nine. You have no other choice, you are dismissed."

"But…," Mr. Harrison tried to say.

"You are dismissed," the President said angrily. "Good day." The President walked away and Mr. Harrison left.

My mom walked into the house and put her things down on the table. It was four-thirty and she just got home from work. She looked through the mail and checked the answering machine but there was nothing of importance. She wanted to hear something about us.

"Did you hear anything," my brother asked.

"Nothing," she answered. "It's the fourth day and they should be back soon." She sat down and turned the TV on. She turned on CNN. Breaking news was flashing across the TV screen.

"This just in," the reporter started. "The President informed us that he will address the nation tonight at nine about Operation Time Discovery and the Time Warriors. He informed us that he is not concerned because they still have one day to go. However, the government is taking all necessary precautions to make sure that they prevent any serious disaster by preparing the rescue team now, so they can leave immediately when they are told. The President also informed us that he wants to make this a regular thing and that he will be addressing the nation more often during Operation Time Discovery. Please stay tuned to CNN for the latest updates and of course the President's address to the nation tonight at nine. Thank you and have a great day."

"Well," my brother said. "That should tell us what is going on."

"Yes," my mom replied as she start toward the kitchen. "But it doesn't mean that the team is alright."

"They are fine," my brother continued as he followed her. "The government wouldn't have let them go unless they felt they were strong enough to handle the mission."

Meanwhile, in paradise, it was dark out and the sky was clear with the stars shining brightly overhead. The four of us were laying in the middle of the field looking at a sky that was much different from the one that we knew. It had the same constellations but you could see the Milky Way Galaxy because there was no light pollution. The temperature was warm and the air was moist with humidity. We could hear the dinosaurs in the woods nearby but we weren't alarmed because they were herbivores. This was the last night we had to spend in this nightmarish yet peaceful place and we were planned to enjoy it. Heather was laying close to me.

"I wonder why the constellations are named the way they are," Heather said. "Do you know what I mean? I mean, why is the Zodiac so important?"

"I don't know," I replied. "But you would think there is a reason."

"Maybe they were giant armies that attacked the Earth and the ancient peoples named the stars after them," Krissy responded. We started to laugh.

"And what about the mystical Atlantis," Heather continued. "I wonder if it really existed."

"What is this," Chris asked. "Asking of the impossible questions?" Heather jumped up.

"And what about the four elements," she continued. "The four natural elements; Earth, Fire, Wind, and Water. Maybe they are the four spirits that created the Earth."

"Yeah," Chris replied. "And they have four hidden temples." He started to laugh.

"Exactly," Heather responded to his smart comment. "And I am an expert of temples on a long, tedious journey to investigate the myth."

"And I'm a rich talk show host," Krissy added.

"Ok," Heather said. "Maybe I'll talk on your show sometime." We all started to laugh. Heather grabbed my arms and pulled me up. "Look," she continued pointing into the open field. "There is the temple of Earth. Let's go inside." She pulled my arm and pretended to lead me inside.

"Look, we found a primitive idiot," Chris said making fun of Heather. "I think all of this tropical air gave her a water logged brain." She ignored his comment and continued to lead me into her imaginary temple.

"And what if my favorite book Brave New World came true," Heather continued. What if a government took over the people and controlled their every move? What if they had assembly lines to create babies and made them to do what they wanted them to do?"

"She really went crazy," Krissy spoke out.

"And what if the people were conditioned like Pavlov's experiment to live their life like the government told them to? What if they were taught things during their sleep?"

"Alright," I said, "I think we get the point." I was getting sick of hearing her talk about these crazy ideas.

"But maybe we can investigate all of these," she said. "Once we are the Time Warriors we'll be able to study all of that."

"If we become the Time Warriors," Chris added. "We have to get out of here first."

"We will," Heather responded. "I know we will." Just then there was a roar. We all stopped and listened. We turned toward the woods. The trees started to sway and then the dino we first met ran out in the field.

Krissy screamed and started running. "Run," I yelled. The dino chased after us. "Head for the trees!" We all ran toward a tree and started to climb it. We sat at the top of the tree. We were too high for the dino to get us but it just stayed there. Then he started to bang into the tree. The tree would move every time that he hit it. He roared and we held our ears. Heather grabbed onto my arm. He ran into the tree and knocked it over. We fell from the tree and landed on the ground with a thud. We covered ourselves as the tree and all its branches crashed down on us. After a few minutes, the dino walked away. When it was quiet for awhile we climbed out. We walked down to the river and followed it upstream to camp. Then we all went in our tents and went to sleep.

CHAPTER TEN

"Good evening," the newscaster on CNN said. "And welcome to the President's speech. We take you now, live, to the White House where the President is about to make his speech about the Time Warriors."

"Good evening," the President said. "I am about to explain to you the entire mission. The whole process of Operation Time Discovery. About five years ago, our leading scientists, led by Dr. Johnson, embarked on a project to create a new machine. They wanted to find a way to send people into time. 'Time', a four letter word created by man, has always plagued our minds with thoughts of far off worlds. As I stand here, I recall as a child playing games where we were far off in a futuristic world. As an adult, we dream of a world that is full of wonderful technology and cures for all the diseases. No matter how far back we look into history, the World was full of the enigma of time traveling. Dr. Johnson and his team were awed by books like Brave New World by Aldous Huxley, which talked about a society that got too advanced. But not just that, the Time Machine by H.G. Wells stunned them even more. At the time it was written, the technology was limited. Yet, Wells describes vividly, a time machine taking a man into a futuristic world destroyed by humans and their technology.

Dr. Johnson and his team decided to embark on the impossible task of creating a time machine to physically send someone through time. The government approved of this project and we granted them the money and supplies they needed. Just months ago they finished the machine and needed to test it.

By their calculations, the machine spins so fast that it finds the time belt. The time belt is a segment of our universe which stores all of history on it. It also holds the key to the future. The scientists created a synthetic element that punches a hole in the space time. The hole becomes a black hole, sucking the machine through a tunnel of darkness. The machine would leave the wormhole and end up in the middle of deep, dark, cold space. The Earth would spin quickly to the time that the machine was programmed and the machine would descend to the surface of Earth.

The scientist felt that they needed to test the machine. They decided that young adults would be the best candidates because they are young enough to be energetic and strong, yet old enough to be responsible and independent. I approved of this, and with the permission of their parents, young adults all around the country competed in state competitions. The winning team from each state competed in a national competition. The winning team of four, Team Pennsylvania, left for the trip just four days ago. They have not returned and we don't know why. We gave them five days as a maximum to study what they wish. However, early tomorrow morning the backup team, Team Missouri, will head into time to make sure the first team is ok. Our scientists are currently tracking the destination of the first team so they know where to send the rescue team. We expect that everything worked as planned, but we are taking all necessary precautions.

If the machine was a success, it will be open to the public for time traveling. If it was not, we will close all projects that deal with it and forget that it was even attempted. If it was a success but it would alter time, then the public would not be allowed to use it. However, if the public is allowed to use it, then the team becomes the new government agency, The United States Time Warriors. I apologize if you feel that you think we are getting to advance and we should heed the warnings of the books that I mentioned, but we have to try. We are embarking on a new revolution in technology and we are doing so as a country. We are the United States of America and we are the world power. Good night and God Bless!"

CHAPTER ELEVEN

Heather and I were sitting on the side of the river. The sun was rising. The sky was orange and magnificent. "This is the day that Danny's team comes to get us," Heather said.

"That's not a good thing," I responded. "I have a bad feeling." I didn't trust Danny. Chris climbed out of his tent.

"What's not a good thing," he asked.

"Danny and his team coming to get us," I told him. He was silent. All I could hear were the sounds of the prehistoric creatures. I grabbed a fruit from the pile that we had and started to eat it. Heather picked one up too.

"What are we going to do about it," Chris asked. "If you are so worried about Danny?"

"We need to build traps," I responded. "And be prepared to defend ourselves."

"I think you guys are talking foolish," Heather added. "There is nothing to worry about. Danny and his team are going to save us, not kill us. You two just talk like typical guys. You are looking for a fight."

"They want to be the Time Warriors," I told her. "They have to get rid of us to get that. So we get ready to defend ourselves." I grabbed a branch from a nearby tree. Then I took a rock and started to make the branch into a spear. Chris did the same. Krissy woke up and crawled out of her tent. When we finished making the four spears I stood up. "Alright, now we need to make a path to follow in case we have to run."

"What are you talking about," Krissy asked me.

"We can have ditches and traps on the path and we will know how to avoid them," I continued.

"What are you talking about," she asked again. I ignored her.

"We make our way to the waterfall, this way we can throw them off the cliff," I informed Chris.

"What is he talking about," Krissy asked Heather.

"He is making a plan to defeat Danny and his team if they decide to attack us," Heather answered her. "It is a stupid idea, they aren't going to attack us."

"Stay here," I told Krissy and Heather as I signaled Chris to follow me. We walked into the woods. I started to dig a hole in the ground. Then I covered it with leaves and dirt. It wasn't deep, just big enough to hurt them and slow them down. Then we made our way to the waterfall. I looked up stream from the waterfall and saw a log stretching from side to side of the canyon. "That's how we get across," I told Chris. "If we need to get across for any reason." He nodded.

"Sounds good," he told me. "This is our territory and we are going to defend it.

57

We earn the right to be the Time Warriors and we are going to defend that right."

"Exactly," I replied. "We defend our territory and our lives." Just then the ground started to shake.

"What is it," Chris asked. "Is it a dinosaur?"

"No," I answered as I searched the landscape. "Its an earthquake! We have to get back to camp." We started to run toward camp. The ground split and we jumped over the crack while it was still small. Just then there was a crack of thunder and we stopped and looked around. The sky was black and the wind was picking up.

"What's going on," he asked.

"I think it is the end," I told him. "It's the extinction." We continued to run toward camp. When we got on the trail that I built the ditch, we jumped over the hole. We finally got back to camp to find that Krissy and Heather weren't there. I looked around.

"Krissy," Chris screamed. "Heather!"

"Heather," I started. "Heather where are you?" I looked all over to try to find some sign of them. Then they came walking out from the nearby woods. "Where were you," I asked. "You scared me."

"We just went looking for you," Heather answered. There was another flash of lightning and then a boom of thunder. It started to rain.

"We need to watch," I told them. "The end is near." Just then the ground rumbled again.

"I don't think the end is near," Chris replied. "I think it's already here."

CHAPTER TWELVE

There was a flash in the sky and I looked up. I saw a bright object close to the atmosphere. "It's a comet," I told the others.

"Well then we better hope Danny and his group get here soon," Heather replied. The sky turned dark and I saw that there were black clouds.

"This is really not good," Chris added. "I don't think we are going to make it out of here."

"Please do something," Krissy begged. "I'll do anything, just get me out of here."

"We're going to be alright," I told her. "I will try all I can but I don't have a time machine." Just then there was a bright flash and a boom. I looked.

"It was just lightning," Heather told me. "Don't worry about it."

"No," I responded. "They're here." I ducked down to the ground. When I didn't hear or see anything, I started to run through the woods to find them. I got to the edge of a field and I could see them getting out of the time machine. It was the same field that we landed in. I ducked down in the bushes and watched them. Then I ran back to camp.

"What was it," Heather asked.

"They're here," I answered. "Get ready. Be careful when running through the woods of our traps. We know this place a little better than they do, so we have the advantage. We have to protect our futures and our lives."

"You have to fight for your future," Chris told us. "If we want this as our future, we have to give it our best fight."

"This is our chance to show them that we are the Time Warriors," I told them. "Let's not fail. After all, we made it this far." I grabbed the four spears that we made. I gave one to each of them. "We wait here," I continued. "Then we lead them on a run through the woods full of traps. There is a log that stretches across the canyon by the waterfall. If we need to get across, that is how we do that." Just then there was a flash of lightning.

"This is like a movie," Heather said. "A huge thunderstorm right before the battle of your life."

"Believe me," I responded. "If we become the Time Warriors, the battles will be worse. Whatever we do, try not to kill the other team. We just need to keep ourselves from getting killed. Then we use their time machine to get home and send another to save them." Danny walked into camp. I got into a fighting stance.

"So this is where you have been living," he said. "I am very impressed." He clapped his hands to congratulate us. I thought you would be dead."

"We were ready for this," I replied. "We are the Time Warriors."

"We'll see about that," he responded.

"Are you ready to take us home," Heather asked.

"No," he answered. "I'm going home; you are going to die. My dad sent us to kill you and then say that we found the time machine in pieces and that there were no signs of you anywhere."

"Really," Chris said. "We'll make sure to tell them your story when we return." Danny laughed.

"You really think you are the Time Warriors" he said. "Don't you?"

"We know we are," I replied.

"We are more than you will ever be," Chris cut in. Danny just continued to laugh.

"Not when your dead," Danny continued. He pulled out his gun. "I think you forgot that we are prepared with our technological weapons."

"I think you forgot," I told him. "That true warriors don't need technology. And we know this place better than you." Danny laughed and shot his gun in the air. Heather jumped and scurried behind me. Krissy backed up. Just then Eric, Erica, and Megan walked in.

"You take Eric," I whispered to Chris. "I'll get Danny." Chris nodded.

"You take Erica," Heather whispered to Krissy. "I'll take Megan." The other three pulled their guns out. Chris and I charged at Danny and Eric and knocked them over. Their guns fell out of their hands and into the river. Heather ran at Megan and knocked her into the river. Then she jumped in after her. They were fighting in the river. Krissy kicked Erica's gun out of her hand and it landed in the water. Erica slapped Krissy across the face. Krissy started running through the woods and Erica chased after her. Eric ran after them and Chris took off to chase Eric. Danny was standing in front of me. He was laughing evilly.

"You will have to do better than this," he told me. He continued to laugh. Just then there was a flash of lightning and the flash blinded Danny. My back was turned to the flash so I took the opportunity to knock him into the river. I jumped in after him. There was another flash. Then another. It started pouring. It was an intense storm, probably the most intense I have ever seen. Danny jumped on my back and pushed me underwater. He held me under and I tried to fight for air. Just then he let go. I pushed to the surface and saw that Heather had kicked him. She was climbing out of the river and Megan was to. Danny followed them. I pushed by Danny and hopped out of the river. Then I grabbed Heather's arm and started running. When we got in the woods, Danny and Megan were catching up. I pushed Heather in front of me. We continued to run. Just then Heather fell in the ditch that I had created. She fell to the ground and held her ankle. I helped her up and we continued to run but she was too slow. They caught up to us in the middle of the woods. Danny knocked me over and I hit the ground with a thud. Just then lighting struck a nearby tree and set it on fire. Megan knocked Heather over. The ground started to rumble.

"Earthquake," Heather screamed.

"No," I said. "It's that dino again. We have to get out of here." The dino popped through the trees at us. Danny and Megan screamed and then ran in fear. I hopped to my feet.

CHAPTER THIRTEEN

I helped Heather to her feet. "Run," I yelled as the dino started to chase us.

Heather couldn't run very fast. I tried to help her but it slowed us down even more.

"Climb a tree," I told her. She started up the tree. I was helping her up the tree. The

dino got to the tree and rammed into the tree. Heather slipped and fell. I hooked my feet

on the branch and hung upside down to catch her but missed. She fell and grabbed on to

the next branch. This tree was tall so we were higher than the dino but he could just reach

Heather. I jumped down and pulled her up right as his jaws snatched at her. He missed,

but we still had to climb to get out of harm's way. The branch we were on had a branch

directly above it. I grabbed it and so did she and we swung many times before we could

catch our feet on the branch. Finally, we caught our feet on the branch and pulled

ourselves up right before he took a bite out of the branch below. We quickly climbed up

to safety. We had no idea where Chris and Krissy were. The dino left in frustration and

we started climbing down. I got my foot caught between a "v" in the branches. She

continued to go down.

"Keep going," I yelled. "I'll catch up." Heather looked up at me and lost her footing and fell to the ground with a thud. "Heather," I yelled. She laid there holding her ankle. I wanted to help her but I couldn't because I was stuck in the branches. Then the ground started rumbling. I looked behind me and the trees were moving. Just then the dino popped out of the trees and came heading for me. I pulled and pulled trying to get my foot loose. The dino kept running for me.

"Hey over here," Heather yelled. The dino stopped dead in its tracks and looked. I also looked to see Heather waving her arms. The dino started toward her and she turned around and headed, limping, toward the camp when in front of her another dino, of the same species, popped out. She turned to the right and another popped out and also from the left. She had four of them surrounding her. I knew we pissed them off enough times and they wanted revenge. They all stopped and she stood in the middle of them. They were interested in her. I pulled my foot loose and headed down the tree. I missed three levels of branches and fell to the ground. I hurried to get up and ran towards them. They were now getting ready to attack. I ran between two of the dinos, grabbed her arm, and pulled her out of the trap and we ran toward the waterfall.

When we got to the waterfall Chris was fighting Eric and Danny. Krissy was fighting Megan and Erica. Heather and I stopped to catch our breath. "You help Krissy," I told Heather. "I'll help Chris." Heather limped over and helped Krissy. I ran over to the log that stretched across the canyon. Chris, Danny, and Eric were making their way to the middle of the log. I hopped up on the log and started to walk across. The wind picked up and the lightning was striking continuously. The ground started to shake. Then the ground by the girls cracked. They all fell in the crack but grabbed on to the edge and screamed. Danny was laughing as Eric and Chris battled. I ran to help the girls. Just then I heard screams from behind me. I turned around and saw Chris and Eric falling toward the river. I ran over to the girls.

"Grab on to my arm," I told them. "One at a time." Heather grabbed on and I lifted her out of the hole. Then I grabbed Krissy and pulled her up. "Alright," I told the other two. "You can either choose to help us get home or die." Erica begged for help. I reached down and pulled her up. She stood with Heather and Krissy. Megan started to slip. "Megan," I said. "Let me help you." She shook her head yes. I bent down to pull her up and she pulled me down. I fell into the crack and grabbed onto the sides. She kicked me. Heather and Krissy each grabbed one of my arms and started to pull me up. I climbed out and went to pull Megan out. She grabbed onto my arm and I started to lift her out. She slipped out of my hand and fell deep, deep, out of sight. I turned around to get hit in the face by Danny.

CHAPTER FOURTEEN

Chris was fighting Eric in the river. Eric punched Chris in the face. Then he grabbed Chris' head and pushed him underwater. Chris tried to fight and push toward the surface. Just then Eric felt great pain in his back. Krissy was in the river and had stabbed Eric through the back with the spear. Chris burst out of the water and gasped for air. "Thanks," Chris said while catching his breath.

"Don't mention it," Krissy replied. "Just get me something to eat." Chris laughed and she did too.

Danny and I were on the log that stretched across the canyon. We each had a spear and we were prepared to battle to the death. Danny ran at me and stopped right in front of me. He swung his spear at my head but I ducked. I stabbed my spear at him but he avoided it. Just then I heard Heather and Erica scream. I looked over and there was a pack of the six foot dinos getting ready to attack them. Danny ran at me as I was watching them and he cut my arm with his spear. I grabbed my arm and stabbed him in the stomach. He fell over. I ran over to the girls and knocked Heather over right as one of the dinos was going to jump at her. It jumped over us. Erica ran toward the canyon and the dinos chased her. She jumped and they jumped after her. They all landed in the water and they attacked her. Heather hugged me and then gave me a kiss.

"We beat our first test," I told her. "Let's go back to the camp." We started walking back to camp. Heather was still limping. When we got back to camp it was dark.

"Do we leave now," Chris asked.

"We need to get to their time machine," I answered. "But I think we should wait until morning. It will be safer to walk in the woods during the day." We ate some fruit and then went into our tents and went to bed.

The picture was getting darker and darker. There was sound of running water. Then of people talking and music playing in the wind. The picture lit up slowly and then there was a view of fresh, clean water running through the streets. People were walking and running on the streets. Everyone was happy. When the picture was fully visible, there were clouds everywhere. And when the clouds cleared, there was an island. It was a beautiful island. But it wasn't just any island, it was an island made of the greenest grass and cleanest streets. It was an island that had no pollution, but yet it had factories. It was an island that had large structures built out of marble and gold. There was transportation methods but they were far more advanced than ever. They had flying cars that ran on water, not gas. Their movie theaters had screens made of water. It was an island that ran on water. Then there were gates in the distance and behind the gates was a giant mountain. And around the mountain ran three rings of water at different levels. At the top of the mountain was a huge temple of some sort. As the gates came closer they read *"Welcome to Atlantis: The Home of Poseidon".* Just then the picture went black again. And when it lit up the city of Atlantis was on fire. There was a tornado and it was being flooded. People were running for their lives. As the picture faded out, all that could be seen was this message: *"The seas raged and the skies thundered. And when the sun rose the next morning, Atlantis was gone. The most talked about society, had become the most talked about myth, to become the most talked about theory, to become the most targeted...".*

CHAPTER FIFTEEN

"**W**ake up," Heather said. I opened my eyes to see her smiling. "Let's go," she continued. "Let's get out of here while we can." I stretched and then crawled out of the tent. I stood up.

"I had the weirdest dream," I told the others.

"What was it about," Chris asked.

"It was about Atlantis," I answered. "I saw it when it was strong and prosperous and then when it was meeting its doom."

"That's strange," Heather added.

"Yeah," I said as I rubbed my face. "But the strangest part is the message I saw at the end of the dream. It said, 'The most successful society met failure in one night. The waters raged and the skies thundered. When the sun rose the next morning, Atlantis was gone.'"

"Weird," Chris said.

"Yeah," I continued. "But still that is not the weirdest part. It said, 'The most talked about society became the most talked about myth to become the most talked about theory, to finally become the most targeted…' and that was it. It stopped there with targeted."

"Bizarre," Krissy replied.

"Can we please go," Heather cut in.

"Yes," I said. We took the tents down and cleaned up the camp to let it like it was before humans got there. The sky was sunny but the comet could still be seen just outside the atmosphere. The earthquakes had taken a break for now. We started to walk through the woods to find the field where they left the machine. Clouds started to build over head.

We ran through the woods pushing the bushes and branches out of our way. Finally we got to the field and stopped to catch our breath. Everyone was excited with joy. Then we looked up and the time machine was gone.

"Where is it," Chris asked.

"I don't know," I replied.

"You have got to be kidding," Heather responded.

"No," a voice said. "I'm not." We turned around and looked. It was Danny with the time machine. I turned to my team.

"You three run for the machine while I fight Danny," I said. "When you start it up, leave. Even if I'm not with you. You don't have that much time left. The comet is going to enter the atmosphere in a matter of minutes. I will try to get to you by the time you leave but if I can't, don't worry about it."

"We can't do that," Heather told me.

"We have to," Chris supported me. "We don't have any other choice." Heather gave me a hug and then kissed me.

"I'll let you say goodbye," Danny said as he laughed. I pushed away from Heather and ran at him. I knocked him over and started punching him in the stomach. The others ran for the time machine. They opened the door and got in. Chris pushed the button to start the machine. Then he put in the time to return them to the present. I continued to punch Danny.

"NO," he screamed.

"Yes," I told him. "Your plan is ruined." The time machine door closed and it lifted into the air and started to spin. He punched me in the face and threw me to the ground. Then he ran toward the machine. I jumped up and knocked him over. I punched him in the stomach where I stabbed him. He cried out in pain. Then there was an explosion from the sky. The comet was flying to the ground. Heather screamed from in the machine. She pressed the "open door" button.

"What are you doing," Krissy asked.

"I have an idea," she answered. A black hole appeared under the machine. "TJ," she screamed. "Run toward the machine." I started running toward the machine like she told me to. Danny caught up to me and knocked me to the ground. "No," Heather screamed in fear. I punched Danny in the face and jumped up again. The machine shot its time energy out and it hit both Danny and I. We were attached to the machine. I knew I was going home, but Danny could not. The comet was about to hit the

ground and Chris hit the warp button. I punched Danny in the face and knocked him out

of the time energy and the comet hit the ground. The machine fell into the warp zone.

The door closed. I was still in the time energy and even though I wasn't in the machine, I

was still warping to the present.

The comet crashed into the ground and the force of the air from it wiped the

entire area clean. It looked like a nuclear bomb hit. Danny was washed away with the

force. I ducked and covered myself as it happened but it didn't harm me because I was

covered by the time energy. Then everything got real black around me. The time

machine had entered space, but I stayed near the surface of Earth.

The sky was dark and there was dust everywhere. I didn't see any life. Then, as

time sped up, the dust cleared and the sky brightened. There was now a clear field around

me with no plants or anything. The canyon was degrading and became a flat plain. Then

the river pushed together and formed mountains. The clouds above me were moving

really fast. Every so often it would rain but only for a matter of seconds. Then I saw the

first seed blow in and land on the ground. Grass began to grow everywhere. Next were

other types of plants, then bushes, and finally trees. Next came small animals like frogs

and snakes. Then came mice and birds. Then came wolves and tigers and hawks. Then I

saw some monkeys walking around. Finally some people were emerging. There was a

wooly mammoth and a saber-toothed tiger running and some early humans hunting them.

Then I saw the ice age. Next came the regeneration of Earth. Then I saw the early civilizations. I floated into the air and around the world quickly. I could see the Egyptians building the pyramids and the ancient Babylonians. Then I saw the rise and fall of the Roman Empire. I saw early wars and the Revolutionary War. Then World War I and World War II. I saw various historical points I have never heard of and even little things like meteorites hitting but not making an impact. I also saw volcanoes erupting and other natural disasters. I saw the building of more advanced technology and an increase in pollution. The waters turned from fresh and clean to dark and dirty. The lands became less and less forested. It was a sad sight to see the whole history of Earth like this. It was depressing to see that Earth was happy and clean until humans came along. Finally the spinning and time warping had stopped and we were in the present.

I stood in front of the time machine waiting for them to open the door. It looked like we were back in the FBI building. The door opened and the others stepped out. Heather hugged and kissed me.

"You made it," Chris said.

"Of course," I replied. "Would you expect anything else?"

"I guess not," he continued. The door of the lab opened and Dr. Johnson walked in. He was happy to see us.

"You made it," he said.

"Of course," Chris replied. "Would you expect anything else?"

"Yeah," Heather said. "After all we are the Time Warriors."

"What happened to the other team," Johnson asked.

"They died in the process of trying to kill us," Krissy told him.

"I had Danny's dad and his helpers arrested," Johnson told us. "So it looks like you four are officially the United States Time Warriors." We all smiled at each other. "You can go home and visit with your families," Johnson continued. "I'll call you with the next step." We all left and returned home.

Heather and her family stayed at my house for dinner and we explained the whole story to our families. They couldn't believe that we survived it.

MISSION TWO:
THE SECRET OF ATLANTIS

CHAPTER ONE

"You're going to have to move to Washington," Dr. Johnson told me over the phone. "Time travel is open to the public so I need you and the other three to move to Washington. I got a few houses in mind. You and Heather can share one. Krissy and Chris can each have their own. Unless you and Heather would prefer to each have your own."

"No," I replied. "We'll share one. We were planning to get an apartment on our own anyway."

"We'll pay for the houses," he explained. "If you give me the confirmation that you definitely want to be the team I'll purchase them today."

"Yeah," I told him. "We definitely want to be the Time Warriors."

"Great," he responded. "I can't wait to work with all of you. I'll put the down payment on the three houses today. I can send some moving trucks if you need help bringing stuff down."

"We'll take care of it," I said. "I think we can handle it. But if we need anything we'll let you know."

"Great, then I'll see you soon. I'll call you when you're needed."

"Talk to you then," I said. He gave me the addresses of the houses. I hung up and looked at Heather.

"We're all set," I told her. "He is putting a down payment on the houses today. He has three houses in mind."

"This is going to be great," she replied with enthusiasm. "You and me on our own. We can finally get some peace and privacy." She hugged me and kissed me with excitement. "I'm going to start packing up my stuff." She walked over to her dresser and started pulling out some clothes.

"I'm going to head to my house," I told her. "I have to gather up my things. We should get to Washington as soon as possible. I figure this weekend we can head down with our families and set up the house."

"This is so awesome," she said as she ran over and kissed me again. "I can't believe we are starting our own life together. I'm not totally excited about having to protect time travel, but at least we'll have a life on our own." I gave her a kiss and walked down the steps and outside to my car. I drove home and started packing my stuff. It was Wednesday and I wanted to leave for Washington on Saturday.

By Sunday afternoon, we had moved everything into the house in Washington. It was a really nice house. There was a huge living room, dining room, kitchen, and three nice size bedrooms and a room for an office upstairs. We had a bathroom downstairs and upstairs. The attic was a nice storage area, and the basement seemed like a good place for a recreational room later on. The walls were white and has some wood trimming around their borders. The floors were hardwood. In between the living and dining rooms was a separation wall with a mirror and stands for putting collectibles. The kitchen had an island in the middle of it with a gas stove.

Johnson had purchased the basic furniture for the house. He had a living room suit including a couch, two chairs, and a coffee table. Heather brought a lamp and stand and she put it in the living room. The dining room had a table with four chairs. There was a hutch with a glass cabinet on top of it. The glass cabinet had three shelves in it. The cabinet had sliding glass doors. The kitchen had four stools at the island. There was a microwave and refrigerator. Johnson had a washer and a dryer put in the basement.

The master bedroom was the only bedroom with furniture. There was a bed and two dressers. A door led to the walk-in closet, which Heather absolutely loved. Johnson also had the office set up. It had a computer on a desk. There was another desk and two chairs. There was a file cabinet and a printer with a built in fax and copy machine.

We settled in and were familiar with the neighborhood by October. There was no need for us at the time so we weren't working. Our jobs were to go into time to protect and regulate time travel and all those who use it. However, there was no immediate need for us. We had to stay in shape, just in case. We trained on our own everyday, and usually went out every night. We would go various places around the city with Chris and Krissy. There was so much to do in the city. Some nights we would see a movie. Other nights we would see a play or go to a football game. Work drug on with really no excitement. We would go to the office and track the registration of time machines. We had people below us in the agency that were responsible for tracking the machines at all times. Heather and Krissy loved the idea that we weren't working. They were happy that we didn't have to time travel. Chris and I were bored with it. We became Time Warriors for the adventure, and this job just wasn't providing us with that. At least not right away.

CHAPTER TWO

It was a rainy, cold, March morning when we got the call. I was so tired that I mistook the phone for my alarm clock. I hit the alarm clock but it didn't shut off. I finally realized it was the phone and picked it up.

"We have a problem," the person on the other line said. "You better get over here as quick as you can." I hung up the phone and rolled over to face Heather.

"Heather," I said softly so I didn't scare her. "We have to go to the FBI building."

"What," she responded. "Why?"

"I don't know," I answered. "They didn't tell me why. They just said to get over there." I pushed her hair out of her face and gave her a kiss.

"Alright," she told me. "Let's go, but that's the last time I stay up that late." I smiled at her and got out of bed. We got dressed and headed down the steps and to the driveway. It was pouring so we got in the car as fast as we could and were on our way.

When we got to the FBI building, Chris and Krissy were waiting for us in the lobby. We greeted each other as we walked down the hall. This place meant so much to us and our adventure; this is where it all started. We got to the door and went in. I looked around and couldn't believe we had done this just eight months ago. We walked down the metal steps just like we did the first time.

There was a flash of light and my mind was venturing into the first time we were here. "There are fifty teams of four teenagers," Dr. Johnson explained. "We have decided that there will be three stages to decide which team gets the ride in time. The first stage will deal with logic. You will take a written test in English, math, science, and history. The teams that fail the test will be eliminated. The remaining teams will enter a stage that will test strength and endurance. Once again, the teams that fail the tests, will be eliminated. The last stage will send the remaining teams through a challenging obstacle course that will require teamwork and all of the skills you used in previous tests. The winning team will get the ride in time. The second team will be a rescue team in case something goes wrong. I came out of my flashback and met the rest of the group where they were sitting.

We were now all sitting in front of the desk waiting for Dr. Johnson. "Good morning," Dr. Johnson greeted us as he came in the door behind us. "You are about to take another mission. I know you didn't have anything to do for eight months, but now there is a need for you. You are going to carry out your first official mission as the Time Warriors. We designed all the equipment and built you a building to work out of. I will join you in that building. I am moving all of my things over there today. However, there will be no time for that right now. Four people left the present last night using a time machine that was not registered. The FBI searched their house and found that they are looking to become rich. They are looking for the secret of a lost civilization."

"Which civilization," Heather asked.

"Atlantis," he replied. "The mystical hydro-city."

CHAPTER THREE

We were dismissed from the room and shown to the new building, which was just down the street from the FBI building. "This building has three floors," the agent said. "Your equipment and training rooms are in the basement along with Johnson's lab. We are standing on the main floor, which contains the lobby, conference room, and break room. Your offices are on the third floor. Dr. Johnson is moving over here today. Have a great day and good luck on your mission." We walked in and went to the elevator. When we got to the third floor, the door of the elevator opened and we entered a hallway. The first office door on the left had Chris' name on it, and across from that was Krissy's. Then next to Krissy's was Heather's and across from that was mine. Chris tried to open his door but it was locked. Krissy tried her next and hers was locked also.

"Now that's funny," I said after trying my door. "He didn't give us any keys." Heather touched the wall and a machine came out. She put her hand on the machine and it painlessly pricked her finger with a needle. A drop of her blood entered through a little hole in the machine and it read her DNA.

"Access allowed," the door said. "Welcome Heather!" We all tried and it worked. My door opened and I stepped inside. Inside the room there was a huge window across from the door. On the wall were plaques recognizing our team for our efforts during the first mission. On the right side of the room, there was a big picture of a black hole. On the left side of the room, there was a picture of the team standing together. On the desk there was a huge and advanced computer system. I sat down and struggled to find the power button. I read the introduction screens and followed directions to put in my passwords and so on. Then I read the screen that explained the basics of this mission. The criminals left last night. I went over to Heather's office and knocked on the door. She opened the door and I went in. All of the rooms were exactly the same. "I saw the mission," I said.

"Yeah, so did I," she replied. "On the computer."

"These are not amateurs we are dealing with," I told her.

"I know," she responded. "But if we survived with the dinosaurs for five days, I think we can handle some crooks."

"Do you want to go check out the equipment," I asked.

"Sure," she answered as we walked out and into the hallway. When we got to the basement, the first door on the right said 'Outfits'. The second door said 'Equipment'. Then there was the training room and Johnson's lab. I put my hand on the wall and the machine came out. The needle pricked my hand, without pain. Seconds later, the machine was reading my DNA.

"Access allowed," the door responded. We walked in and there were huge glass cases and inside each was an outfit. There outfits were the same as the ones we wore on the experiment. There were black jeans with a white T-shirt that had 'Time Warriors' inscribed in black on the pocket. The shoes for the guys were black boots and for the girls they were black heel boots. I walked up to the case and looked in. I tried to open it by banging on the glass, but it wouldn't budge. Just then Heather pushed a button on the wall and the glass case surrounding the outfits sunk into the ground. We were now able to get to the outfits.

"Wow," Heather exclaimed. "That's really cool." We got dressed and then looked around the room. I saw some belts and they were black in color with a silver square in the middle. I hooked one on my waist and Heather did the same. We headed to the third floor and instructed Chris and Krissy to get dressed. The four of us, all in outfit, met in the lobby and sat down. Heather and I sat down on the couch and Chris and Krissy each grabbed a chair. I put my arm around Heather and she rested her head on my shoulder.

The lobby was huge with glass windows making up the front of the building. They were tinted so the sun wouldn't shine in. It was busy, with secretaries and other people bustling around the desks in the middle of the lobby. The chairs and couch were located on the right side of the lobby against the wall. The pattern on the furniture had clocks with different times on them.

"We're going to have a meeting in five minutes," Johnson instructed us as he walked by with his equipment. "In the conference room."

"I just can't believe this," Heather said.

"What," I asked.

"Here we are," she replied. "I'm eighteen years old and part of the newest government team. We just graduated from high school and tested the first ever time machine. Now we are the Time Warriors and expected to watch over the public use of time travel."

"It's amazing isn't it," I responded.

"It's dangerous," she told me. "You're the leader don't you realize this stuff?"

"You're my girlfriend," I comforted her. "Chris is my best friend and Krissy is my cousin. I won't let anything happen to you guys." Chris and Krissy smiled at us and nodded their heads.

CHAPTER FOUR

We all met in the conference room and Dr. Johnson came in. "I am instructing you on this mission so that you get use to the way it works, but from now on this will be TJ's job. He is the leader and so he will hold the meetings about the missions. You four will need to leave for Atlantis very shortly. Heather and TJ make sure you load up on equipment before you leave. Krissy and Chris you will have to figure out how to work the communication equipment. I am going to continue unloading my equipment and bringing it into the lab."

"Do you need help," I asked.

"If you don't mind," he replied. We all helped Johnson unload and set up in the lab. Then we went to work on the mission. Chris and Krissy went into Chris' office and turned on his computer.

"Now we have to figure out how to work this stuff," Krissy said.

"It can't be that hard," Chris told her.

"It is when you have a moron leading the process," Krissy replied.

"You're not leading," Chris responded to her comment. "I am."

"I would be better off as leader of this little mission," she told him. "At least I'm not dumb."

"No you're dumber," Chris replied. "And besides, the only mission you can lead is one that leads to food."

"Shut up," Krissy snapped. The computer was loaded up and Chris sat down in his chair.

"If I click on this," Chris said to himself. "Then this, oh maybe this."

"Do you like talking to yourself?"

"Yeah, when no one is around. The only thing here with me is a beast that can't speak English." Krissy slammed her hand down on his desk and looked at him.

"I am going to hurt you," she told him.

"Am I supposed to be scared," he asked. "The only hurt you can do is when you sit on someone."

"Why I ought to," she started.

"I got it," Chris screamed with excitement. "I figure it out and it works."

Heather and I walked into the equipment room. The walls had shelves on them and on the shelves were smoke bombs, mini-bombs, long shots, and lasers. Then I saw some helmets and leather jackets, both were silver There was a huge garage door and I pressed the button to open it. Inside were two motorcycles and they were silver and black.

"Those could come in handy in the future," I said. We gathered up the equipment we felt we needed and headed back upstairs to our offices to meet Chris and Krissy. Johnson walked in to the my office, where we were all located.

"I want TJ and Heather to take a motorcycle and go to the house of the criminals," Johnson instructed. He handed me a piece of paper with the address on it. "They left, but I want you to see if you can get any information about what they are after that they may have left at their house." Heather and I walked out of the office and to the elevator.

"Here we go," Heather said with a sigh. We made our way to the basement and to the motorcycles. We each put a silver leather jacket on and a helmet. The helmets were really cool, a mix of silver and black like the bikes. I got on the bike and Heather got on behind me. I started it up and drove out of the building.

CHAPTER FIVE

We got off the bike and I started to walk around the outside of the house.

"Follow me," I said to Heather when I met up with her. We walked to the side of the house. The house was a big brick building with two windows in the front, and one on the side. There was a porch with a swing on it. It looked like a normal family house. The window on the side, which I was now trying to look in, had white curtains. I looked in but all I saw a light on.

"Someone is home," Heather cried.

"People leave their lights on when they leave," I told her.

"I don't know about this," she continued.

"Let's go inside," I said. Every time I told Heather we were going to do something, she looked uneasy. We walked to the back door and I turned the knob, but it was locked.

"What do we do now," Heather asked. "Can we go home?"

"No," I answered. "We find another way in."

"Oh, wonderful," she said sarcastically. "More sneaking." I looked at the base of the house to see if I could get in a basement window, but there was nothing. I pulled the long shot off my belt and shot it up to the roof. I climbed onto the roof and looked around. There was still no way in. "Look at the attic," Heather instructed. "There might be a way in." She shot her long shot up and boosted herself up on the roof. Then I laid down on the edge of the roof and looked down into the attic window. Nothing, so I took the laser and cut the window out of its frame. I put the window on the roof and slid down off the roof and into the window.

"Come on," I said to Heather. She slid down and into the attic. I saw a chest with a lock so I cut it with my laser and looked inside the chest. It was old clothes and junk. "Damn it," I yelled as I slammed the chest lid down."

"What," Heather exclaimed. "You have to be quiet someone is going to hear us."

"No one is home," I told her. "But I don't think they would leave any information laying around anyway."

"There has to be information here," Heather replied. "Johnson said the FBI found it."

"That's what the criminals want us to believe," I added. "They made fake plans to throw the FBI off their tracks. You don't think that if they went through all that trouble to steal something from Atlantis, that they would leave the plans in their house. Besides, if the FBI is so great why didn't they stop the criminals before they left?"

"Well," she commented. "Let's look around anyway." Just then I heard a crash outside. I ran to the window that we came in. The window that I cut out fell off the roof and shattered on the ground. The back door opened and a woman in her thirties stepped out. She was medium height, with blonde hair, blue eyes, and she was skinny.

"Shit," I said softly to myself. "They are home." She looked up at the attic and I stepped away from the window.

"Nice going," Heather responded. "Way to be smooth." I looked at her and shook my head. I heard someone coming up the steps and we jumped up on the ceiling boards and crouched down. The attic door opened and the woman came in. She looked around and then left. As soon as I heard her go down the steps I jumped down and Heather followed. I opened the attic door and peered down the steps. There was no sign of anyone. I took the walkie-talkie off my belt and signaled Chris.

"Yeah," Chris said.

"They're home," I told him. "We are still going to explore the house as much as possible. But keep an eye on the time tracker to make sure they don't leave."

"Right," he replied. "Be careful if they are still there." I put the device back on my belt.

"Let's go," I told Heather, "downstairs." She shook her head and followed me quietly down the steps. When we were on the second floor, we found another flight of stairs. I signaled Heather to stay there and I started down the steps. I saw four people sitting in the living room. I snuck back up the steps and looked at Heather. "They're all sitting there," I told here quietly. I walked around and she followed until we found another flight of stairs. Again, I snuck down and saw that it led to the kitchen with the light off. I signaled for Heather to join me and we continued down into the kitchen.

"Get me a soda," I heard a man say.

"Ok," a woman replied. "Do you want some chips too?"

"No," he replied, "just a soda." The kitchen door swung open and I signaled Heather to follow me. We slid behind the island that they had in the middle of the kitchen. She kept the light off and I was glad because we weren't as obvious in the dark. She opened the refrigerator and grabbed a soda. She was petite with brown hair and brown eyes. She walked toward us so we scurried to the other side of the island. "Tori," the man yelled with anger. "Can you hurry up?"

"I'm coming Matt," she replied. "Jason, do you want anything?"

"No," a voice replied. She walked out of the kitchen and into the living room. I saw a door and I ran over and opened it. It was the bathroom, then I tried another and it was the closet. Finally I saw a door in the back of the kitchen and opened it. It led to the basement and we followed the stairs down into the darkness.

"I wish they would give us a flashlight," Heather told me.

"That's something to talk to Johnson about," I replied. There was nothing in the basement of interest to us. We ran up the steps and out the back door.

"What do we do now," Heather asked me.

"Well, we wait here and see when they leave," I told her. We sat down by the porch, but behind some bushes so we were covered. She laid her head on me and we fell

95

asleep because we were tired from the night before.

CHAPTER SIX

I was woken up by a static sound. I checked my walkie-talkie and found that it was making the noise. It was getting light out and I knew it was early morning. We must have slept through the night. "TJ," I heard, "are you there?"

"I'm here," I replied.

"TJ, they left," Chris said.

"What do you mean they left," I asked.

"They left," he answered. "They must have left during the night. We fell asleep here and didn't see it until now."

"We fell asleep too," I told him. I got up and shook Heather and she woke up.

"What," she asked as she stood up and stretched. Then she brushed herself off.

"They left," I said.

"You woke me up for that," she said. "They probably went for groceries. I mean who cares?"

"No, they left for Atlantis," I continued.

"Then let's go," she replied.

"All we have to do," Chris told us, "is hit the button on our belts. It works just like the time machine except it is easy to carry."

"Are you serious," Heather asked.

"Yes," Chris answered. "Johnson created them this way so it would be easier for us."

"Then we're going back in time for the second time," I said.

"Ok," Chris replied. "Let met get Krissy." It was a few minutes before he came back. "Ok, we're ready," Chris informed us.

"Alright, on three," I told them. "one, two,…"

"Wait," Krissy cut in on her walkie-talkie. "On three or after three?"

"Three," I ignored her question. It felt like something took over my body. We programmed in the time and place just by saying it out loud. Then it was calm for a second. Heather and I looked at each other as the ground began to shake and fade away. A big, black hole started to form and the wind picked up. Then suddenly it pulled us in and the next thing we knew, we were flying through a tunnel in deep blackness. Chris and Krissy met up with us in the wormhole. It was really loud with all the wind. Then a light came into view and when we reached it, we shot out into a silent, cold area of space. I could see my breath as I looked around at the stars. I looked to the left and saw the Earth. It started to spin counter-clockwise. It got faster and faster as we just floated in space. It became a blur because it was spinning so fast and then it just stopped. A few seconds later we fell toward the Earth at an amazing speed with fear crossing our minds. We entered the atmosphere and a bubble came around us to protect us from the friction. We continued to fall very fast and I was getting worried that we weren't going to stop. However, we slowed down and floated to the ground.

CHAPTER SEVEN

I looked around at the island and saw that it was huge. In the middle of the island, was a huge mountain. The mountain was separated into three parts by large two bodies of water. We were in front of the entrance gate. I walked up to the gate and knocked. The gate opened and a man stepped out.

"Nu wa snuga," he mumbled.

"Do you speak English," I asked.

"Ye yag wala," he continued. All of a sudden, a whole line of soldiers were standing in front of us pointing their spears at us.

"Unlike the first mission," Chris exclaimed. "This time I didn't do it."

"Maybe they're welcoming us," Krissy added.

"I don't think that's the welcoming committee," I responded. "Run!" We took off toward the wall and started to climb it. We stood on top of the wall and looked at the army, now outside the gate.

"YAA," the man that opened the gate yelled. The spears came flying up at us and we jumped off the wall and into the city. We took off running down the street with the soldiers on a close pursuit. I heard music everywhere and the grass was greener than green. It was warm and sunny with a slight breeze, with the smell of ocean. The streets were diagonal from the shore and there were canals of water with boats throughout. As we were running, three flying cars flew over us.

"Wow," Chris exclaimed. "They have better technology than we do." The army continued to follow us and we were watching them. A sewer gate opened and we fell down into the hole. We were sliding down this tunnel-like structure that just twisted on and on. It was really dark and we couldn't see how far it went on. When we hit bottom, I stood up and looked around. We were standing in a dark, dungeon-like room with candles all over. The candles, in fact, were the only light source. I saw a figure in the darkness and it came closer. As I squinted, I could see it was a young man about our age.

"Welcome," he said.

"How do you know how to speak English," Krissy asked.

"We invented the English language," he replied. "But no one uses it yet. However, I watched you from the gate and heard you speak English. You looked like you could use some help. I don't normally help intruders but you looked familiar."

"I don't think we've met before," Heather said. He walked over to her and grabbed her hand and kissed it.

"My name is Atlanton," he told her in a sexy voice. He was about six feet tall, like me, with silver hair and turquoise eyes. He was wearing pants that were metallic blue. He didn't have a shirt on and I could see that he had a tattoo on his arm, but I wasn't able to see what it was.

"I'm TJ," I interrupted him. "And this is my girlfriend Heather, my friend Chris, and my cousin Krissy."

"That's great," he cut in. "Heather, I know more about this island than anyone else. I spend my time exploring and learning about it. Would you like me to show you around?"

"Sure," she replied with enthusiasm. I shook my head in disgust and followed him as he led us down a tunnel.

"This is an underground passage system used for the royal family,' he told us. "I learned how to sneak around down here. The royals don't use it anymore anyway." He led us to a ladder and we climbed up out of the sewer. There was a canal with a boat waiting at the dock.

"Where are we going," Heather asked him.

"I am going to show you the story of Atlantis," he told her. "As it is told to us." He led us to the boat and pointed to a building in the distance. "That's where we are going," he continued. The island was beautiful. The water was crystal clear with fish swimming in it. He paddled us to the building and I felt like we were in Rome or some other romantic place. The building was made of marble and huge. We walked up to it and I stared in awe.

"What is this," I asked.

"This is city hall," he answered. I still heard the music and wondered what it was.

"What is the music for," I asked.

"The music is caused by the wind hitting the aerodynamic domes the buildings have for roofs. It is constantly playing because if there is no wind, it is caused by water pressure."

"That's unbelievable," Heather cried. "This place is so beautiful."

"Not nearly as beautiful as you," Atlanton added. Heather blushed with the flattery. "Now follow me." He led us in the building and down a hallway. He motioned us to stop and so we did. "Sit," he ordered and we did. Then he lifted his arms into the air in front of him and a screen was created out of water. "The story of Atlantis," he said. The screen wiggled a little and then 'The Story of Atlantis' appeared in writing on it. A clouded world appeared and marble buildings were sitting on the clouds.

"At the beginning of time," the screen explained. "The gods were living their lives in a beautiful paradise. Everyone shared in the chores and entertainment. However after time, war broke out and the gods fought amongst themselves. Zeus, the king of gods, decided that they were bored and that was the reason for them fighting. To solve the problem, he decided to allow each of the gods to create a paradise on Earth. They could create it however and wherever they wanted to. Hades, the god of the underworld, created a dark and gloomy place way below the surface of the Earth. He thus became the god of death and decider of your death date. Zeus stayed in the heavens and ruled all paradises. It was Poseidon, the god of water, who created Atlantis. Poseidon came to an island in the middle of a large body of water, which he later named the Atlantic Ocean, and stepped foot on what would be his home. He was bored on the island so he created a race of people from the ocean's water. That race became the Atlanteans. He fell in love with one of the women he created and was given eleven sons, ten of which would become kings. He divided the land into ten kingdoms and let ten of his eleven sons rule those kingdoms. Meanwhile, he created a temple for the Atlanteans to use in their worship to him. The eleventh son was banished to an ordinary life for all time. However, the ten sons fought amongst themselves for full control of the island. One of the kings, King Atlas, had the other nine murdered. He was never convicted of the horrible crime and even today is the ruler over the entire land. The people of Atlantis respected the land and created a flourishing civilization." The screen shut off.

"So what happened to the eleventh son," Krissy asked.

"No one really know," Atlanton answered. "We assume he is part of our society, as a regular. Now if you follow me, I'll get you something to eat and show you a place where you can sleep." He took us back to the boat and back into the sewer, if that's what it really was. He led us down a tunnel to a large room. "This is where I live and you are welcome to stay here for however long you like. For whatever reason you are here, my instinct says you are here to help us, so it doesn't matter." He put a bunch of fruit and vegetables on the table and left. We sat down and started to eat.

CHAPTER EIGHT

As we were eating, I was thinking about some of the stuff Atlanton had said. Then I turned to the group. "What if the criminals are after the Temple of Poseidon," I said.

"Yeah, ok, the brought a disassembling crew with them," Krissy replied.

"No, he might be right," Heather said. "That is the center of Atlantis and they could be after the thing that holds the city together."

"Who asked you," Krissy snapped at her.

"We don't need to be asked to talk," Chris told Krissy.

"You're not even in this conversation," Krissy responded to him.

"I was just trying to help out Heath…" he tried to finish.

"Yeah," Heather butted in. "You're not even in this conversation. I don't need you're help anyway."

"Well," Chris exclaimed. "Excuse me!"

"Why do you need to be excused," Krissy added. "Just leave. No one is stopping you." I sat back and waited for the arguing to stop.

"Krissy, all you ever do is disagree with everyone," Heather said. "TJ leads this group and he is smart enough to know what they might be after."

"Oh, I forgot," Krissy replied. "He is the all-knowing genius."

"No," Chris cut in. "He just knows what he is doing."

"Shut up Chris," Heather continued.

"Sorry," Chris replied.

"Alright," I yelled. "We're not enemies. We need to concentrate on stopping the criminals." I walked down the tunnel and climbed up the ladder and out onto the street. Chris went exploring the sub-terrainian tunnels. Krissy followed Chris without him knowing and Heather sat at the table.

I stopped at a canal and looked into the river. It was so clean and I couldn't believe it. A soldier snuck up from behind me and cracked me across the head with a metal bar. I fell over and hit the ground unconscious.

"So why are you here," Atlanton asked Heather as he joined her at the table.

"Huh, oh we came to visit," she answered.

"Yeah, right," he replied. "Like I am supposed to believe that."

"It's true," she defended her statement.

"How did you get here," he asked.

"A time machine," she said.

"Where do you live," he asked.

"America," she answered.

"Where's that?"

"It isn't close to here."

"Is it on another planet?"

"No, just in another time. It isn't discovered yet."

"Where is your boyfriend?"

"He's up exploring."

"What! He left!" He took off running and climbed out onto the street. He saw the army standing in a circle around me. He floated into the air and his eyes lit up. "Let him go," he ordered. The army looked at him as he created a huge wave of water behind him and used it to wash them away. He landed on the ground and helped me back to his kitchen. "Don't leave this protected area," he instructed me. "The army wants you dead for intruding."

"How did you do that," I asked.

"I have some special powers," he said.

"Do all Atlanteans have that power," I asked.

"No, only certain ones," he replied. He walked into his room and Heather and I followed. I looked around and saw that he had walls made of water with fish swimming in them. He had water molecules suspended in the air. He had a waterbed and his desk was glass with water in it. He took a white T-shirt out of his dresser and put it on. Heather snapped her fingers in disappointment. I looked at her in shock and she shrugged her shoulders.

"What," she cried. "Can't I look? The guy is hot, his chest is perfect and now he is covering it. I am disappointed, ok?"

"Whatever," I replied.

"This place is really strange," Heather said. We went to the kitchen with Atlanton and met Chris and Krissy.

"We need to start looking for some people we know," I told Atlanton.

"Where do you want to start," he asked.

"The nearest jewelry store," Heather answered.

"You got it," her replied. "A beautiful piece of jewelry for a beautiful lady." She smiled and pushed his shoulders. He led out of the sewer again and down the streets toward the jewelry store.

CHAPTER NINE

When we got to the jewelry store, we went in. "Heather," I said, "You and Krissy distract the sales people. Chris, help me look around for any clue you can find." Heather went up to the saleswoman.

"Hi," she said. "Can you help me find a certain jewel I am looking for? I am trying to find a present for my friend." Krissy was working with the other saleswoman.

"Sure, look here," she answered Heather as she pointed at the display case. She started explaining various jewels.

"TJ, I found something," Chris said. I walked over to him and saw the note from the criminals.

Dear Time Warriors,

We are after the secret of Atlantis and we know you don't have a clue as to what it is. Well, now you do have a clue. Although we want to meet you face to face, we are not going to tell you what it is. We will however leave you clues to follow us to the secret and then we will beat you. This way, we can have some fun playing with your minds. Here is your first clue, a poem from us to you.

Most criminals aim for this
it is that which causes society to crank
It just can't be missed
it holds the object that they wish to yank

I looked up at Chris and tried to figure out what they meant. "What does it mean," Chris asked.

"I don't know," I answered. "We have to figure it out."

"Good idea," he said with enthusiasm. "I didn't think of that." We signaled the girls and left the store. I handed the note to Heather and she read it out loud.

"What makes society crank," Krissy asked. "They want to steal food?"

"No," Chris took advantage of the opportunity to bust on Krissy. "Only you crank on food."

"Society cranks on the same thing that criminals wish to steal," Heather explained. "They're headed to the bank."

"Take us to the nearest bank," I told Atlanton.

"You got it," he replied. When we got to the bank I searched all over for the next clue. I looked up at the ceiling and saw a piece of paper so I used my long shot to pull it down. I opened it and read it.

Time Warriors,

> **How's it going? It's going great here! Here's your next clue.**

Until next time!!!!

We walked back to Atlanton's house and sat down at the kitchen table. I tried to crack the clue as I sat down.

"What does all of this mean," Krissy asked. Atlanton walked into his room and returned with a huge crystal ball-type thing.

"What the hell is that," Krissy asked.

"This is going to help me see what the criminals are after," he answered. "But first, I want to see what qualities you each hold." He took his hand and rubbed it over the surface. Water appeared in it and it was swirling around. "Place your hand on it," he instructed me. I took my hand and carefully placed it on the ball. "I see a moon," he explained. "You are the moon because you are the leader and you watch over your team during tough and dark times. Just like the moon watches over the Earth during the night." He turned to Chris and signaled him to do the same. "Put your hand on it," he demanded. Chris did as he was told. "I see a falcon," Atlanton told Chris. " Like a falcon, you are strong, swift, and brave."

"Awesome," Chris exclaimed.

"Now you, Heather," Atlanton said as he smiled. She hesitated for a moment and then walked forward and put her hand on the ball. "I see a lark," Atlanton told her with a smile. "I see that you are beautiful and graceful like a lark." Now he pissed me off one too many times.

"You do know she's my girlfriend," I yelled.

"Yeah well," he replied. "I can't help it, that is what the crystal ball says."

"You're full of shit," I muttered as I made an angry face. He ignored my comment and expression.

"Ok, Krissy," he continued. "Your turn." Krissy walked forward and placed her hand on the ball. "I see eight of you."

"What does that mean," Krissy asked.

"Now," Atlanton ignored Krissy. "Let me see where the criminals you are after are at the moment." He placed both his hands on the crystal ball. I looked into it and saw the island of Atlantis. He was searching the entire island.

"What does it mean," Krissy screamed. Atlanton was still ignoring her. Krissy walked over and pushed past Atlanton. She picked up the ball and threw it across the room. Atlanton created a wave and caught the ball in it.

"What is you're problem," he screamed at her. "I can't get another one of these things. It is one of a kind. The only one made."

"Then answer me next time," she said forcefully. "What does it mean that you saw eight?"

"It means eight," Atlanton answered.

"Why would you see eight of me," Krissy asked.

"Because you are the size of eight hippos," Chris replied.

"Why I should…," Krissy yelled at Chris. "Come here you punk!"

"I didn't make it up," Chris tried to defend his comment. "The ball did."

"Oh boy," Heather complained. "Here we go again." Krissy chased after Chris and I stopped Krissy.

"Knock it off," I ordered.

"It means that you will be extremely important for this team," Atlanton told her. "You will carry the load of eight people." Chris laughed at the thought of Krissy being important.

"She already carries the load of eight people," Chris said laughing. "Look at the size of her and tell me that isn't true."

"Shut the hell up," Krissy fired back. "At least I'm not a stupid bird."

"Enough," Heather cried. "We have to worry about catching the criminals."

"We can worry about that tomorrow," Atlaton told us. "It's getting late so I think we should get some sleep." He led us down the tunnels to a room. "This is your room," he said. He immediately walked out of the room. "If you need anything," he continued as he walked away. "You know where I am." He left and Krissy and Chris ran for the beds on either side of the room. Heather and I got stuck on blanket on the floor. We all laid down and Chris and Krissy fell asleep quickly.

"This place is pretty cool," Heather whispered.

"Yeah, but I liked the dinosaurs better," I replied.

"You don't like Atlanton do you," she asked.

"Is it that obvious," I responded.

"Don't let him get to you."

"I know but he is trying to win you and the group over."

"Now you know that won't happen. We only follow you."

"I know but he's cooler, smarter, and different and you said yourself that you like different."

"You can't compare yourself to him, he's from a different time period. And besides, I love you."

"He doesn't seem to concerned about the criminals. Does he?"

"Don't worry about it tonight." She leaned over and kissed me. "Goodnight."

"Goodnight," I said and before I knew it I was sleeping.

CHAPTER TEN

"**A**hhhh," I screamed as I woke up. I was breathing heavy. "Nightmare," I told

myself. I looked to my side and saw that Heather was gone. Chris and Krissy were still

sleeping. I stood up and stretched. I looked around the room and then walked out and

into the hallway. I searched the hallway for signs of Heather, but nothing. I walked down

the hallway to Atlanton's room. I heard Atlanton and Heather talking so I stopped outside

his room and leaned against the wall.

"So, TJ is your boyfriend," Atlanton said.

"Yeah," Heather answered. He took his shirt off and stared at her. I was ready

to charge in there but contained myself. "Maybe I should...," she tried to say.

"Sit down," Atlanton told her as he pointed to the bed. She listened and sat

down and he moved to stand in front of her. He leaned down to kiss her but she pushed

him away. I was ready but I trusted Heather and didn't want to have to break that trust.

He pushed her down on the bed and climbed over her and started to kiss her.

"What the hell are you doing," I screamed as I ran in. "Back off!" He stood up

and backed away from the bed. I walked over and grabbed Heather's arm and took her back to our room. "Get up," I yelled to Krissy and Chris. They jumped up and I kicked them out and slammed the door. "No competition, can't compare," I yelled. "Isn't that what you told me last night."

"Calm down," she cried.

"Calm down," I yelled. "Do you know what you were doing? I wonder what was going to happen next?"

"Nothing happened," she continued to defend herself. "I went over to talk to him and he took his shirt off. Then he tried to kiss me and I pushed him away. He pushed me down on the bed and kissed me. Then you ran in, that's where it stopped."

"I know," I told her. "I saw the whole thing. Why didn't you fight back?"

"You were spying on me," she cried.

"Yeah," I answered, "and I am glad I did."

"How could you," she claimed.

"How could I," I screamed in shock. "That's what you say about the situation? How could you just sit there and not do anything?"

"Exactly," she answered. "We didn't do anything. And besides, I told you, he's hot. He had his shirt off and I was stunned. If a girl did that to you, you wouldn't be able to push away either."

"I could if it meant it would hurt you," I responded. I stormed out and slammed the door. She opened the door and followed.

"TJ, wait," she yelled as she ran to catch up. Atlanton came out of his room and

I grabbed him by the shirt and pushed him against the wall.

"Leave my girlfriend alone," I screamed in his face.

"Maybe she doesn't love you," he replied. I went to punch him but Heather grabbed my arm.

"Stop it," she cried. "Stop it! I'm sorry. Just don't hurt him."

"If he wants a fight," Atlanton said. "We'll take it outside."

"Bring it on," I yelled.

"No," Heather screamed. "I won't let you do this."

"It is too late," I told her. "He asked for it."

"He wants this fight," Triton replied. "He is going to get it."

"This is ridiculous," Heather continued. "You two are acting like immature boys. I'm sorry. Just please don't hurt each other.

"I'm not going to hurt him," Triton told her. "And he certainly isn't going to hurt me."

CHAPTER ELEVEN

Outside Atlanton ran at me and knocked me down. He started to punch me. I punched him in the face and threw him off me. I climbed to my feet quickly just as he was running at me again. I moved out of the way and he ran past me. I ran to him and kicked him in the chest. I punched him in the face and then he tripped me. I fell to the ground and hopped right back to my feet. A crowd was gathering around us and I didn't pay attention to them. Heather was screaming every time one of us looked like we got hurt. Atlanton grabbed a metal bar and swung it at me and I ducked. I jumped up on a box as he swung it at my feet. I grabbed a bar also, the bars were like long metal staffs. I swung it at him and hit him in the knees, causing him to fall over. I ran over to him and grabbed his arm. I saw the tattoo on his arm.

He pushed me away and I looked at him. He got back up and cracked me in the face with the bar and I fell over. He ran over to me and put the bar on my chest. I looked up and didn't have the strength to move.

"Looks like I win," Atlanton said with pride. I kicked him off me and got up. I picked up the bar I was using.

"I don't think so," I replied with confidence. "You'll have to do better than that." I ran at him and he flipped me over his back and I fell in the river. He started to laugh and Heather ran over and pushed him in. He grabbed onto her and pulled her in with him. Chris ran over and jumped in. The crowd looked at Krissy and she hid her face as if she didn't know us. Atlanton grabbed Heather in the river.

"So I see that you chose your boyfriend," he said. "Well you won't have one when I'm through with him." She slapped him across the face. He made an angry face and threw her backwards in the water. I swam over, underwater, and took his legs out and he fell backwards into the water. Chris helped Heather out of the river and climbed out himself. Atlanton held me under and I was fighting to get up for air. I punched him in the stomach and he let go of me. I swam quickly to the surface and gasped for air. He came after me again and grabbed me by the neck and threw me backwards. He created a whirlpool in the water and I got sucked in.

"This guy doesn't know when to quit," Heather said. "He's going to kill TJ."

"That's the point," Chris replied. "They battle to the death over the girl." Heather ran for the river but Chris stopped her. I was under the water stuck in the force of the whirlpool. Heather pulled her long-shot out and Atlanton saw it. He created a wave and knocked her and Chris down. Then he took the wave and pushed the long-shot

119

into the river. Heather grabbed Chris' off his belt and shot it to me and pulled me to shore. She helped me out and laid me down as I was gasping for air.

"Are you ok," Heather asked. "Are you hurt?"

"I'm ok," I answered catching my breath. Heather got angry and got in her ticked stance.

"Oh-oh," Chris cried. "Atlanton's in trouble." Heather walked over to Atlanton and looked in his eyes. Chris ran over and pulled her away. "You won," he told Atlanton.

"Good," Atlanton replied. "I always do.

"But I am still staying with my boyfriend," Heather said furiously. He walked back to his house and then we did. We got back to our room. I remembered the tattoo.

"His tattoo," I told them. "It's the same symbol as our last clue."

"But what does three triangles pointing to three symbols mean," Chris asked.

"I don't know," I said. "Three of the symbol maybe but what does the symbol mean?"

"What about something to do with angles," Chris asked.

"That doesn't make sense either," I answered.

"What about three angles," Krissy asked.

"I don't think that's it," I responded. I walked over to the counter and saw a book with their language on it. I opened it and saw that it was a book that converted their language into English. "Here's the alphabet," I told the team. They all walked over and looked at it. "It's converted to English. Afterall, Atlanton claims that the Atlanteans created the English language." Heather looked at it.

"The symbol in the middle says 'ton'," she replied.

"Three tons," I continued. "Why would he have that as his tattoo?"

"You said three tons," Heather said. "What if you use the three prefix 'tri' and put it with 'ton' to get 'triton'."

"That's sounds good," I said. "The question is what is triton?"

"Think about the story," Heather told us.

"What about the ten kings," Chris said. "Do they have anything to do with triton?"

"No, I don't think so," I replied. "The only king that sticks out in my mind is Atlas and he didn't have anything to do with triton. He is the surviving, sole-ruling king that murdered the others."

"What about the stick thingy that they use," Krissy asked. "What's that called?"

"A trident," Chris answered. "You idiot."

"I'm just trying to help," Krissy replied.

"Well don't," Chris told her.

"How about the eleventh son in the story," Heather said. "Does he have anything to do with triton. Atlanton said he doesn't know what happened to him."

"That could be his name," I said. "Hey, that's it. Atlanton is the eleventh son banished by Poseidon and his name is actually Triton. I had my suspicions from the beginning but now this proves it." I walked out of the room and to Atlanton's room. He was laying on his bed listening to music with a device much more advanced than a CD player, it ran on water. I walked in and he jumped up off his bed.

"Look, I know you're mad but...," he tried to say.

"I'm not after you," I replied. "I want to know why you lied to us?"

"What do you mean?"

"I mean that you are the eleventh son, Triton."

"What? How did you figure that out?"

"That's our job, now what would the criminals want with you?"

"I don't know, why do you ask?"

CHAPTER TWELVE

I went back to the room and the others were sitting around. "I confronted Triton," I told them. "He doesn't know what they want with him." I laid down on the floor and Heather came over and joined me. Chris and Krissy were laying in their beds and we all fell asleep.

I woke up and looked around as I tried to orient myself to believe that I was still in Atlantis. I had a nightmare about 'paradise'. I looked around the room and saw that the others were still sleeping and I stood up. I walked quietly down the tunnels and out onto the street. It was dark out, probably early in the morning and no one was around. I looked up at the mountain and saw two rings of water around it. Then at the very top I saw lights and I began to wonder what it was.

"What are you looking at," someone startled me. I turned around quickly to see that it was Heather.

"Oh, you scared me," I replied. "I'm wondering what those lights are up on the mountain." She put her arms around my waist and rested her head on my chest.

"That's the temple of Poseidon," she said as she smiled at me. "Remember?"

"Oh, yeah," I answered. "I forgot."

"This place is beautiful," she continued."

"Yes, it is," I agreed. "But I can't believe how advanced they are."

"I know," she added. "They are even more advanced than us."

"Yeah, they even have flying cars," I replied. "And buildings that make music in the wind. Canal systems that are so advanced they wouldn't be thought of for thousands of years, or so historians say. But what really happened to this place?"

"They got to advanced," she answered.

"If that is possible," I replied, "then we are heading in that direction."

"Or maybe they got too greedy like the story says," Heather continued.

"I think we did that already," I told her.

"Let's go in," she responded. "It's not safe to be out here." She looked up at me and gave me a kiss. We went back in and back to sleep.

CHAPTER THIRTEEN

The next morning I went out to the kitchen and met Triton sitting at the table.

"Have you ever been to your father's temple," I asked Triton.

"Yeah of course," he replied. I asked him this because he lied before so I wanted to find out the truth.

"Well," I continued, "the criminals want something with the temple. What could they be after?"

"Maybe my father's statue," he replied.

"They can't move the whole statue," I responded.

"I don't really know then," he told me. The others came out and met us at the kitchen table.

"There is only one way to find out," I continued. "We have to go to the temple."

"It's quite a hike," he told us. "We have to climb three inclines and swim across two lakes."

"We do what we have to do," I told him.

"Alright then," he said. "We'll go. But don't say I didn't warn you!" He walked into his room to get ready and we all did the same.

Not too long after the conversation, we were on our way up the first incline. The inclines had houses on each side and people in the street. The canals ran through the allies between the houses. Some houses were even built over running water and we thought that was pretty cool. By the time we reached the first lake, we were all pretty much tired.

"This is nuts," Krissy complained as she tried to catch her breath.

"Suck it up," Chris commented.

"Stop it," I demanded before they could even continue.

"This is the first lake," Triton explained. "It is the bigger of the two. The second and third inclines are not as bad as this first one. Basically, I am saying that it will only get easier." He took his shirt off and threw it on the ground and then headed into the lake. Chris and I followed his lead and then the girls decided they didn't have a choice. We were in the middle of the lake when something strange started to happen.

"There is a shadow below me," Chris said. "And it doesn't look nice."

"Keep swimming," Triton explained. "As fast as you can."

"What is it," Krissy asked. Just then a giant water snake drove its head out of the water and hissed at us.

"Holy shit," Chris screamed. It grabbed Chris with its tail and swung him into the air.

"Do something," Heather yelled at Triton.

126

"I think you forgot to mention something," I said to Triton. Triton ignored our comments and created a sword out of water in his hand.

"That's going to do a lot," Krissy cried with fear. "You're going to stab the snakey with water."

"Hu la yu ya wacha mala," Triton yelled with anger in his voice. "Heche yocha noka!" A cold wind came over the lake and the water sword froze into a sharp blade of ice.

"That could work," Krissy commented. He used his powers to shoot a geyser at his feet and he flew into the air. As he came down he did so head first with the sword out in front of him. He drove the blade into the snake and the snake squealed in pain. The snake threw Chris and I swam over to make sure he was all right. Triton pulled the sword out and drove it into him again. He continued to do so until the snake was no longer moving.

"I'm freezing," Heather cried. The water of the lake was starting to freeze over.

"Hurry to shore," Triton ordered. "This spell takes a long time to wear off and the lake will freeze." We made it to shore and stood on the beach warming up in the hot sun. I looked back at the lake and saw the storm clouds still over the lake. Yet where we were standing, it was beautiful and warm. Triton walked over to Heather and rubbed her shoulders as she was shivering. Everyone looked at me and I just ignored what Triton was doing.

"Can we get moving," I said to break it up. "It might be easier to stop the criminals before they steal whatever they are going to steal."

"Let's go," Triton picked up after my complaint. He led us up the second incline, which had fewer houses and more canals. This was much easier than the first incline and we got to the second lake very quickly.

"I'm not going in there with the snakey," Krissy put her foot down.

"Will you stop talking like a two year old," Chris commented.

"There are no snakes in this lake," Triton told us. "This time there are man-eating fish." We all looked in fear and he laughed. "I'm kidding," he continued with a chuckle. "There is nothing in this lake. We hardly even see a snake in the first lake, it just so happened that it was out hunting today."

"You better not be lying," Heather told him.

"I'm not," he replied. "I couldn't lie to such a beautiful lady. Besides, I've crossed this lake thousands of time and never saw anything." He made his way in and we followed. We were across the lake in a few minutes. It was much smaller than the first one and he was right, there was nothing in the lake.

"That was easy," Chris said with confidence.

"Stay close," Triton ordered. "And keep quiet."

"Why," Heather whispered.

"We don't want to disturb the holy ground protectors," he told her.

"The holy what," Krissy yelled. "Do you mind speaking up!"

"Shh," Chris threw back. "Will you be quiet…" Before he could finish there was some movement from all sides of us. "Just great," Chris continued. "Why is it always Krissy that screws things up? I think we should leave her at home next time."

"This is really not good," Triton yelled at Krissy.

"Oh shut up," she replied. "Just use your freakin' powers and stop crying like a little girl."

"They are going to strip me of my powers," he told her. "And they are much more powerful than me." I looked and saw them standing on the sides of us ready to attack. They were made of rock and very strange creatures.

"What do we do," Heather said as she looked at Triton and then me.

"Fight them off as we run for the temple," Triton replied. They charged at us and we began battling them off as we moved slowly toward the temple. One started slashing its sword at me and I kept avoiding it. Triton raised his arms and created a wave to wash them away but they shot a beam of light at him and the wave disappeared.

"What happened," I asked.

"They took my powers," Triton replied. I punched one in the stomach area and shook my hand in pain.

"We can't fight them," Chris yelled as he was trying to avoid getting stabbed by the sword. "They are too strong."

"If we make it to the steps of the temple," Triton replied, "they won't be able to harm us."

"They are slow," I yelled to them. "If we run, we can definitely out run them."

They all nodded their heads and we ran for the temple. Then to our surprise, a line of the holy protectors appeared at the steps of the temple.

"I forgot that they would do that," Triton told us. "I only had to battle them once before."

"How did you win," I asked.

"When they killed everyone else I was with, I managed to slip away," he answered.

"What do we do now," Heather asked.

"We have no choice," he answered. "We have to fight them." He looked at Chris and I. We charged forward at them and started battling with them. The one I was fighting grabbed me and threw me backwards. I landed on my back on the ground. I stood up and brushed myself off and ran back to the front line. Krissy and Heather just looked on. "Run for the temple," Triton instructed the girls. They did just that but two of the protectors grabbed them. Chris and I ran over and kicked the protectors with all of our strength. It was enough to get them to release the girls. Heather and Krissy made it to the steps of the temple and a beam of light shot out and the protectors disappeared. Chris, Triton and I then made our way up the steps and to the doorway of the temple.

CHAPTER FOURTEEN

Now that we had the holy protectors defeated, we stood on the steps of the temple and looked up at it. "This is one big temple," Chris said.

"It's big because it represents the creator of Atlantis. My father, Poseidon," Triton replied. "This temple is protected by four warriors. They will be unleashed if you touch anything. So here's a tip, don't!"

"Krissy," Chris added as he looked at her.

"How dare you accuse me of screwing things up," she replied. "I never did!" Chris laughed at her comment.

"It doesn't matter," Heather cut in. "Just nobody touch anything!"

"We can go in," Triton continued. "But first I want you to meet my girlfriend Valorian. Valorian means 'strong and courageous' and she watches over the temple during the day. There are people that take shifts looking over the temple and she is on right now." Valorian, an attractive girl met him at his side. "Alright, let's go in," Triton said as he walked up the steps and in the door.

"You never told me you had a girlfriend," Heather complained. "That's not very nice."

"I'll hold up the rear," Chris said. I followed Triton and Valorian with Heather at my side.

"That's where you belong," Krissy replied to Chris. "Cause your an a…"

"Don't even," I cut in. "It isn't necessary." The temple was made of marble with gold scattered throughout, just like the rest of the buildings.

"This is awesome," Chris said. "It is huge. How are we supposed to find the criminals in here?"

"We usually do it the old fashioned way," Valorian said.

"What's that," Chris asked.

"You look," Triton added. Krissy laughed at their attempt to make Chris look like a fool.

"Thank you for the new technique," Chris commented. "I didn't realize you were that advanced."

"I didn't realize you were that stupid," Triton replied.

"Duh,' Krissy responded to Triton. "Like where were you this whole time?"

"Shut up," Chris snapped back at her.

"Knock it off," I ordered. Triton led us down a hallway and in the first door. Inside there was a huge statue of Poseidon holding a trident on his chariot being pulled by six white horses. I walked over to the statue and picked up the note that was laying there.

Hello Again Time Warriors,

   This is your final clue to the secret, good luck (you'll need it)! Keep your

eyes open. *ατλαντισψ*

   "What is that supposed to mean," Chris asked.

   "Like I know," I replied. "I can't read Atlantean."

   "Duh," Krissy responded. I looked at her with anger and she backed up.

   "I can," Triton responded. "It says Atlantis and has my father's symbol at the

end of it."

   "But why would they give us a clue that says Atlantis," I asked.

   "It is the Atlantean code for Atlantis," Heather responded. "Therefore, they're

after the Codes of Atlantis." The criminals walked into the main chamber room where we

were standing.

   "Now that you know what we are after," Matt said, "I guess this is where it ends.

We get the codes and you get to die!"

   "I don't think so," Chris replied. "You can talk a big line but can you walk it?"

   "Let's find out," Tori replied

   "Bring it on," Krissy added.

   "What do you want with the codes of Atlantis anyway," Heather asked.

   "They only hold the key to creating a rich and powerful society," Matt answered.

"I don't know, you tell me why we want them?"

"Well you're not going to get them," Chris said firmly.

"We'll just see about that now won't we," Matt continued.

CHAPTER FIFTEEN

"**I**s anyone else shivering," Chris asked. "Because I'm shaking so hard I think I might be having a seizure."

"So you really want to fight," Matt asked.

"No," Chris answered. "I'm making fun of you for absolutely no reason except my health."

"Alright," Matt responded. "Have it your way."

"I'm scared now," Chris exclaimed. Matt whipped out a switchblade. "Ok, maybe I'm scared now," Chris continued. "How about you guys?" He looked around at us and then at Triton. "Uh, Triton, a weapon please!"

"Why would I carry a weapon," Triton asked him.

"I don't know. Why are you asking me," Chris answered.

"Because you asked me first," Triton replied. "And besides, I have my powers."

"Oh yeah, I forgot," Chris continued. Matt chased Chris down one hallway and Tori ran after Heather in a different direction. Jason followed me as I followed Heather. Triton and Valorian stood right by the statue and couldn't believe what they were watching. Krissy followed Chris and Sara followed her. Krissy caught up to Chris and jumped on his back and caused him to fall face first to the floor. They got up, turned around, and Matt and Sara were standing in front of them. The room was filled with weapons on the wall and in glass cases.

"How do you want your organs carved out," Matt asked.

"How about in their shapes," Chris answered. "Can you do that?"

"Just use a knife," Krissy replied. "I'm not too picky."

"I'm sure I can arrange a few shapes," Matt replied.

"Great," Chris continued. "Here's an idea, draw them in your head."

"Actually, I need practice," Matt replied. "I am thinking about becoming a surgeon."

"There she is," Chris said as he pointed to Krissy. "She is the perfect person to practice on."

"Hey, I'm not a woman," Krissy said as she looked at Chris and winked. "You'll have to find a true female."

"You think you're smart," Matt continued. "Don't you? Well I have news for you, you're not." He ran toward them and Sara followed his lead. Chris and Krissy ran the other direction back to the main chamber room.

Meanwhile, the four of us were now upstairs in the temple. It was a tribute to Poseidon with a lot of pictures. Pictures of Atlantis and of the heaven's, pictures of the kings and the Atlanteans graced the walls. Heather kicked Tori in the head and she stumbled backwards but Jason caught her. Jason threw me backwards and I fell to the floor. Heather ran over and kicked Jason where it counts and he dropped to his knees and let out a high-pitched scream. I grabbed Heather's arm and we ran back down the steps toward the main chamber.

On the way to the main chamber, Krissy saw a gold dagger with three blades on the wall. She stopped, backed up, and grabbed it. Moments later we all met in the main chamber and Triton and Valorian were still standing there. We all stood by them and Krissy used the weapon to draw a circle around us.

"Don't think about crossing that," Krissy told the criminals.

"Yeah, don't cross…that…," Chris said reluctantly. "Krissy, where did you get that?"

"Over there on the wall," she answered.

"We're dead," Chris replied.

"No we're not," Krissy answered. "We're still standing here."

"Now we know what Americans are like," Triton told Valorian.

"Don't use those two as an example," Heather told them.

"What did Triton say as we walked in this place," Chris asked Krissy.

"I don't remember," Krissy answered.

"He said don't touch anything," Chris screamed at her.

"Oh yeah," Krissy replied, "but I didn't. I just touched the gold spikey thingy."

"Yeah," Chris told her. "The trident. And where was it? I don't think you pulled it out of your back pocket."

"You know, you're right," she continued. "It was on the wall over there. But I thought I told you that already?"

"And what happens now," Chris asked her.

"I don't know, what," she responded as if she was burnt out. "All you do is ask me hard questions."

"The big guys come and they kill us," Chris explained.

"Oh, yeah," Krissy replied, "I forgot, the big guys come and they… WHAT?"

"They kill us," Chris told her. Just then there was a crash and the four statues in the room were breaking open. There was a statue in each of the corners.

"Thanks, Krissy," Heather cried.

"If we make it out of here alive," Chris continued, "remind me to give you a huge pat on the back!"

"No problem," Krissy replied. "I'll remember."

CHAPTER SIXTEEN

Now Heather and I stopped to ponder what we should do next.

"Guys, I have one word of advice," Chris said.

"Now what," Heather and I said at the same time.

"Run!"

"Good idea," I replied. We ran to the right while Valorian and Triton stood there. We ran down the hall and saw a giant water army coming toward us so we started the other way. We ran right past Triton and Valorian and they just shook their heads. When we got in the left hallway we saw the four guards walking toward us. We walked backwards to Triton.

Chris started to run toward an open hallway with a door. The water army was following right behind him. He ran in the room and put a giant block in front of it. He looked for a weapon. " A weapon. A weapon. Where am I going to get a weapon?" Chris said out loud to himself. "I would use this staff on the wall but it would awaken the statues. Oh yeah, Krissy did that." He grabbed the staff off the wall and pulled the block from in front of the door and opened it . The water army multiplied so he slammed the door shut and put the block back in front of it. "I'll just put this right back where it belongs and they'll disappear. I hope." Just as he put it back another fell off the wall. "Crappy," he cried and decided to put it back which caused the rest to fall off the wall. "Stop falling off the wall. What am I going to do?" Triton walked through the wall. "How did you do that," Chris asked.

"I have the power," Triton replied as he moved the block from the door.

"Hey, what are you doing? Are you nuts?" Chris exclaimed with fear.

"Relax it's under control," Triton replied.

"Relax. Under control. There's about fifty billion water soldiers out there and you want me to relax."

"Shut up Chris."

"Yes Sir." Triton opened the door and his eyes lit up. He floated into the air.

"Das ist nicht so gut," Chris exclaimed as he backed up. The army moved closer. Triton lifted his arms and the wind picked up. He threw his head back and a big wave appeared behind him. His arms, still in the air, kept the water controlled.

"This will teach you to mess with someone weaker than you," Triton said angrily.

"Hey, I resent that," Chris cut in.

"Get ready to surf," Triton said to the army as he swung his arms forward and the wave went flying out at the army and washed them away. He landed on the floor and kicked the door shut. "Grab a mop," he said to Chris. "Let's clean this place up."

Meanwhile in another area of the Temple, Heather and I were busy with our guards. Heather went one way and I decided that if we split up it would make it easier, so I went a different way. I ran down the hall and to a room. The guard followed me in. He pulled out a staff and started to swing it at me.

My guard swung the staff at my head but I ducked. Then he swung it at my legs so I jumped over it and kicked him in the stomach and he stumbled backwards. He dropped the staff and came running at me. He pushed me into the wall and I was a bit dazed. He started to punch me in the stomach. Then he threw me to the other side of the room and I landed in a bunch of boxes. I kicked him and he flew backwards into a glass case and got cut open but he got right up. Water came out from the cut and in seconds it was gone.

"Just great," I thought. "He's made of water." I picked up his staff and started to beat him with it. He kicked me across the face and I fell backwards. He grabbed the staff and pressed a button on it, and a knife came out. He placed it on my chest by my heart.

"Time to die," he said. "And I'll sacrifice your body to Poseidon." He lifted the staff up.

"Hey. How about you don't," a girl's voice said. "Back off." He stopped, looked around but saw nothing. He turned back to me.

"What kind of games are you playing," he asked. He heard something and turned around and a girl jumped down and kicked him in the face. Her eyes lit up and she

141

floated into the air and created a huge tidal wave. The guard and I got sucked under but the girl helped me out. The guard disappeared.

"Thank you," I said. "My name is TJ."

"I know who you are," she said. "I've been following you. My name is Auriana."

"Why did you help me?"

"I am an old friend of Triton's. Now let's go." We left the room.

Meanwhile over in another room Heather was preparing to fight her guard. The guard ran at Heather and kicked Heather in the stomach. Heather flew backwards with a thud against the wall.

"Ha ha ha you are so weak." She grabbed a staff off the wall and ran at Heather as if to stab her but Heather grabbed the staff and flipped the guard over her head and onto the floor. She stepped on the guard's stomach.

"Now who's the weak one?"

The guard flipped Heather backwards. Heather hit the ground and laid there motionless. The guard jumped up in seconds and grabbed two daggers. She swung them at Heather. Heather jumped up and grabbed two daggers also. The guard tried to stab Heather but she moved backwards and twisted around and cracked the guard in the head with her elbow. The guard slashed at Heather but Heather blocked it with her daggers. Heather tried to stab the guard but she moved. Then she swiped her daggers at Heather and cut Heather's arm. Heather grabbed her arm to stop the bleeding. Just then Triton walked in the room and ran over to Heather. He grabbed her around the waist and looked at her arm as she passed out. He lifted his arms and his eyes lit up. He floated into the air. A geyser of water shot from the floor at the guard but missed. The guard clapped her hands and a statue in the room woke up. It was made of rock and was some kind of bull-like thing.

"Poseidon wants to have some fun," the guard said. "And he has fun by watching his little boy get killed by a rock. Oh, and no powers." Just then a stream of light came down and stripped Triton of his powers. The rock thing just came toward him and he kicked it in the face but hurt his leg. The rock thing punched him in the face and he flew backwards into the wall. Just then Valorian ran in to help but the guard cut her off by kicking her in the stomach. The guard grabbed a dagger and stabbed Valorian in the chest and she fell over. Heather grabbed a dagger and while the guard wasn't looking she stabbed her. The guard fell to the ground. Just then I ran in and kicked the rock thing in the back and he turned around. Heather snuck up behind him and placed a bomb from her belt on him. I waved goodbye to him and he blew up. Triton got up and ran over to Valorian.

"No," he cried. "Why her? She had nothing to do with this."

"I'm sorry," I said.

"Leave me alone," he replied. "Just get out of here." We did as he asked. We walked away quietly.

CHAPTER SEVENTEEN

Meanwhile, Chris was fighting his guard in a hallway. He ran at the guard and knocked him over. The guard pushed him off and hopped to his feet. Chris got up and ran at the guard again. This time the guard moved and Chris went flying through a glass case and laid motionless. Chris pulled his laser out and shot it at the guard. The guard screamed in pain as the laser cut through his skin. Water came pouring out of his wounds and he fell to the ground and became a puddle. Chris stood up and brushed himself off and looked at his cuts.

All that was left was Krissy's guard. And she was being taken care of at the same time by Krissy. "Welcome to my turf," the guard said. She ran at Krissy and Krissy screamed. This was a battle of scaring each other and not of violence.

Meanwhile upstairs, Heather and I were walking when we stepped on a loose tile and we fell through and landed on Krissy's guard, killing her. We walked, with Krissy, back to where Triton was. He was still laying there crying.

"Is there anything we can do," I asked.

"Yes, leave me in peace," he said.

"I am so sorry," Heather said as she hugged him. "I never meant for her to get killed. None of us did." We walked out of the room and down the hall. We went to the chariot room. I was thinking about how selfish I was to allow them to get involved in our problems. I was also wandering how we were going to find the Codes of Atlantis without Triton's help.

"Alright," I said. "The least we can do is stop the criminals from getting the codes."

"I don't think we should. Haven't we cost enough pain," Heather said.

"Look, I know we caused that loss of Triton's but we at least need to prevent another," I continued. They agreed so we continued to walk down the hall. Triton came running up to us.

"Guys, wait," he said. "I need to help you so I can prevent myself from another loss." Just then a huge blue bubble surrounded us and carried us to the chariot room.

"Now that was dumb," Krissy said as she sat down on one of the horses.

"Well, hello," the statue said. Krissy jumped up in fear.

"Father," Triton said.

"Yes, son, it is me," the statue said as Poseidon became alive. "I am about to tell you the story of you. You were born on a cold rainy morning. It was January, yeah, January twenty-fourth. The minute I saw you I knew you were different and were going to be able to save Atlantis in your own way. I made you an outcast to have you prove to yourself that you were strong enough to do anything. When you were just a baby I put you on your own. I watched you grow up and develop into a handsome, bright, strong, and courageous young adult. I've seen you handle your life and survive. However, I needed a real test and you passed it today. You put aside your emotions and physical well being to help complete strangers and that showed me you were mature. If you can stop the criminals, with strangers, I will make you a god. Auriana I see you standing over there." She looked at him and smiled. "TJ, I bet you didn't know Auriana is Triton's sister. If you help them to Auriana, I will make you a Goddess. Now go, defeat the criminals." The living statue became dead once more.

"So what are we waiting for," I said. "We have a God and Goddess in the making." We walked down the hall and down the steps to the basement. I was leading the group. It was dark and cold. I could barely see anything. I grabbed the candle on the wall and lit it.

"Here you lead the group," I said to Triton as I handed him the candle.

"No you're a better leader," he replied.

"Don't you just love him," Heather exclaimed as she hugged me and kissed me on the cheek.

"No, not really," I mumbled under my breath.

"What," Heather asked.

"Nothing," I answered. I led them down through the tunnel but I couldn't find anything. There was a branch off so I took it and still there was nothing.

"Let Triton lead," Heather said. "You haven't found anything."

"Yeah really," Krissy agreed.

"What do you think Chris," I asked.

"You've been leading us around and we haven't found a thing so I think that Triton should take over too," he answered.

"Ahh," I screamed as I punched the wall. Triton came up aside of me.

"Sucker," he said quietly. "Your girl is in love with me and your jealous." I gave him a nasty look and moved to the back. Auriana came up next to me.

"Don't worry about them," she said. "I think you're a great leader." Triton led us down a different tunnel. We finally got to the part of the Temple where the Codes of Atlantis are stored. We walked in and saw a huge golden statue of a muscular man holding a green ruby with codes in many languages on it. Auriana read the sign on the wall to us in English.

WARNING:

He who should disturb the codes of Atlantis will not leave the island alive and will perish with the rest of the population.

"That doesn't sound good," Chris said.

"It's not good," Triton said. "It means if someone should touch it the whole island will die off. And I have a feeling the criminals don't realize that.

"I have a feeling that they don't care," I added.

147

CHAPTER EIGHTEEN

We heard some rustling down the hall and saw some light. We stood in the corners like statues. The criminals walked in and looked around.

"Yes, we have it," Matt said. "We finally have the Codes of Atlantis and those little pipsqueaks aren't here to get us."

"Excuse me," Chris said.

"What," Matt asked as he turned around to see who it was.

"I'M BBAACCKK," Chris answered as he turned around and punched him in the face.

"I don't have to worry," Matt said as he regained himself. "I brought some friends."

"Huh," Chris claimed with a confused look on his face.

"That's right," Matt continued. "I brought two powerful Atlanteans and about twenty water soldiers."

"Oh great," Chris said. "More fun!"

"Hi Triton," an Atlantean said as he entered the room. "Long time no see."

"Deron," Triton gasped with shock. "What are you doing with them?"

"I found out you were here so I took the opportunity to beat you again," Deron answered. "For the last time."

"Funny, but I don't think you beat me the first time," Triton exclaimed.

"Heh, you have that much confidence in yourself," continued Deron.

"Yeah, actually I do when I fight a person as weak as you," Triton replied. Matt sent the water soldiers after Chris and the other Atlantean after me. Chris ran down the hall but didn't get far when he got caught and thrown against the wall. They formed shackles out of water and pinned him to the wall with shackles around his arms, legs, and waist. The other Atlantean, a girl named Kanena, chased after me. She formed a huge bubble out of water and sent it after me. I got caught in it and tried to break out but it was pointless to try because it was impossible. The criminals took Heather, Krissy, and the Codes of Atlantis and ran out of the room.

Triton and Deron were left to fight so they had a power battle. Deron punched Triton and pushed him backwards into a wall. Deron raised his arms and formed a wave. He sent it toward Triton and Triton tried to fight for his breath. Triton used his spell to turn the wave around and sent it at Deron. Triton started to overcome Deron but Kanena ran over and hit Triton in the back of the head with a metal bar. Triton fell to his knees and was knocked out. Auriana was standing behind the statue the whole time and ran out and sent a wave of water at Kanena and Deron. The water swallowed them and she chanted a spell. The water froze and they were trapped in it. She ran over and helped Triton up, then they ran down the hall. They met me in the hallway where I was still trapped in the bubble.

"Go get the criminals," Auriana said to Triton. "I'll help TJ." Triton took off and Auriana burst the bubble. I fell to the ground and gasped for air. I took a few minutes to catch my breath. Auriana ran off to help Triton. I stood up and ran over to help Chris.

"Just go," Chris yelled. "Stop the criminals from getting out of the Temple."

"I can't leave you here to die," I replied. "I have to help you."

"Don't worry about me," he continued. "If you don't stop the criminals, I will die anyway. And so will a lot more people." I agreed with him and was on my way.

Meanwhile, the criminals were just getting to the chariot room. When they got in there, Poseidon's statue woke up.

"I won't let you leave this island alive," he said. "Even if it means the death of my people and son and daughter."

"Who are you," Matt asked.

"I am Poseidon. The Water God and ruler of Atlantis," the statue answered.

"Forget it Matt," Tori said. "It's them trying to play a trick on you."

"You're right," Matt said as he took off running again. Krissy and Heather were not too happy with being captured and they tried to free themselves but Jason had them handcuffed to him. As soon as they left the chariot room, the temple began to shake. The doors of each room had steel bars on them and they started to close.

"This is not good," Heather said to Matt. "It's not us. It's the gods."

"Shut up," he said with anger. "You're just trying to scare me. And if I want your opinion I will ask for it." They continued on their way out of the temple as I caught up to Triton.

"TJ, go down the hall, to the left and out the door," he said. "It will take you to a passage that will lead you out of the tunnel. If you stay with me; you will die. Get out of here."

"No, I will not leave," I told him. "If my teammates die; I die."

"Get out of here and come around the front of the Temple. You may be able to stop them that way."

"No. We go this way and hope a door stops them." We continued to follow the criminals. Back down in the basement Chris was still chained to the wall. He knew he was going to die so he closed his eyes and waited. Auriana walked through the wall in front of us and she started running with us.

"We have five minutes," she said, "if we're lucky until the Temple floods." Finally we got to the main chamber. The criminals were there and they stopped for a second. Poseidon closed all the doors so they could not get through. We were on the outside of the chamber and could not get in.

"Great," Sara said. "What do we do now?"

"If we are going to keep Heather, let's make some use out of her," Matt said.

"What are you going to do with me," she asked.

"Just use your skills to get us out of here," he answered.

"If you touch her you're dead," I said. He put his hand on her belt and pulled off the laser that was clipped to it.

"I saw you use this laser to cut through things," he continued. "I'll use it to cut the bars." He took the laser and cut the bars in half and then on the bottom and on the top. Then he took the handcuffs off of Heather. "Go," he said to Heather. "Push your way through and make sure it is safe."

"If you're so strong and courageous why are you having her do it instead of yourself," I said. He pushed her through the bars and she went in. There was rock door blocking the tunnel. She tried to get it opened but she wasn't strong enough.

"I can't get it," she said.

CHAPTER NINETEEN

"You are so weak," Matt said. He stepped over the bars and pushed Heather out of the way. She fell on the floor on the outside of the bars. Matt kicked the rock and busted it open.

I took the laser off my belt and started to cut the bars. I could here the water in the tunnel behind us. Tori, Sara, and Jason went through the passage and out of the tunnel. I finished cutting the bars and started to break them.

"Thanks for the help," Matt said to Heather as he slapped her across the face with his staff. She fell to the floor and held her face. I got through the bars and ran in and punched him. He hit me back and grabbed the Codes of Atlantis. He started to run but I tripped him and the Codes flew out of his hands. Jason looked back in and saw the Codes in the air. He ran and grabbed them. Auriana helped Heather up. Jason took the Codes and stepped out of the Temple.

"Nooo," Triton screamed in fear. "This can't be the end!" The ground began to shake and explosions were heard in the background. We all ran out of the Temple. I looked behind us at the mountain and saw that it was erupting. A thunderstorm with heavy winds came above us.

"I have to go back for Chris," I said.

"No use," Triton explained. "The island is about to be destroyed, and you won't have enough time. Besides he's probably dead by now." We started to head back down the mountain. I could feel the mountain shaking with the pressure of the water. It started to rain and the lightning was intense. I grabbed Heather's arm and Triton led Krissy and Auriana down the mountainside. Lightning struck right in front of us and a tree fell in our path. We jumped over it and continued to run. A tornado was in the distance and the sky was getting darker and darker. We were on the third level of the island. We still had to climb down the second and first level and make it through the city to the gates. The mountain was filled with lava. The tornado was ripping down trees and either the water was rising or the island was sinking. We got to the first moat and swam across to the second level.

Meanwhile back in the Temple, Chris was still chained to the wall. "Man, it's awfully quiet in here," he said. Just then he felt something cold on his feet, he looked down and saw water. "Oh shit," he cried. The room he was in was one of the last rooms to get flooded so most of the Temple had to be flooded by now. "Now would be a good time for you guys to come save me," he said. "If I die, you die, remember? Somebody. TJ, Heather, Krissy please help me! Help!!!!"

We continued to run down the second level. The island started to shake and I noticed it was sinking. We ran faster, trying to avoid people and buildings and taking the

154

shortest path, but it seemed as if it went on forever. When we finally reached the second

moat we swam as fast as we could across it. Triton figured he could help us go faster so

he created a wave to push us across the moat. When we got across and were on the

second level, we weren't that far from the city. Just then fire fell from the sky. It was

gigantic fireballs and they were hitting the ground constantly and everything was catching

on fire. One almost landed on me but I rolled out of the way. We continued to dodge

them as we ran.

The water was up to Chris' chest. "Oh, that's cold," he said. "Somebody help

me," he was screaming. "Anybody."

When we got to the city the buildings were on fire. People were left lying in the

streets. The water was up to our ankles. It seemed each step made the water get higher.

When we got about three blocks from there the water was up to our knees. It was getting

complicated to run. Another three or four blocks and the water was up to our waist. Now

we could only swim because the water was too deep to walk.

"That's cold," Heather said. We continued our way toward the entrance gate.

The fireballs continued to fall but were put out immediately when they hit the water. One

hit me and lit me on fire but I went under the water and put it out. By now the water was

up to our chest. The storm was getting more severe. When we got to the entrance gate, it

was closed and the water was just about over our heads. I pulled on them but they

wouldn't open because of the water. We climbed up the wall and over. Just then the

storm kicked up a huge wave and pushed the entire island under along with us. A blue light formed around Auriana and Triton and they disappeared. Heather, Krissy, and I got sucked under and I tried to fight to get to the surface.

The temple was the last thing to go under because it was on the mountain but it did go under. Chris was now really scared. Just then a girl swam in and grabbed him. She pulled him out of the Temple and through a secret passageway that led to the roof. She pulled him to the surface and they gasped for air.

Meanwhile, despite our efforts we were going further down. Suddenly I saw Heather and Krissy start to go towards the surface. Triton was pulling them out of the water but I was still going down. Then I saw Auriana coming down towards me and I passed out from the loss of air. She got to me and put her hand around my waist and started to swim toward the surface. When we got to the surface she gasped for air but I did not. Triton punched me in the chest and I gasped for air. Chris met us with the girl that rescued him.

"My name is Anelica," she said.

"That must mean angel," Chris told her.

"Yeah, actually it does," she replied. "How did you know that?"

"Because you are my guardian angel," he replied as he kissed her. Triton created a small island for us to stand on. The storm had died down and the sky was clearing. It was like it had never happened. The sun was rising in the east and there was a bright orange sky.

"Thank you," Triton said. "For everything you did for us." Just then a bolt of light came down and Auriana and Triton rose into the air. Valorian met Triton in the air and they hugged. I just smiled. "If you ever need me, I'll be there," Triton said. "I promise to look after you." They rose up until they disappeared above the clouds.

"Let's go home," I said as I got ready to count to three. "On three., one...two..."

"Wait," Krissy said. "Do we press it on three or after three?"

"Whatever," I said. "Who really cares any more? One...two... three." We pushed the button on our belts. The ground began to shake and fade away. A black hole formed behind us and the wind picked up. Finally, we got sucked in and flew through the deep dark tunnel.

"Haven't we had enough tunnels," Heather yelled. Then we saw the bright light at the end. We shot out into the dark, cold, space and saw the Earth. It began to spin clockwise. It got faster and faster. It was spinning so fast I couldn't see it. Then it stopped and we fell to the surface. When we arrived at the surface one of the agents was there to greet us.

"I want to hear one thing from everyone to make sure your ok," the agent said.

"That was really cool," Krissy said. "And Triton was cute."

"I can agree with that," Heather said. "I'd like to meet him again."

"The criminals are dead," Chris explained. "So where do we go next?"

"One selfish act took place, and by dawn, the most advanced society was gone," I said. "I just can't believe it happened."

MISSION THREE:

MASTER OF TIME

CHAPTER ONE

Three weeks had passed since we returned from Atlantis. Krissy packed up her things and left after quitting. Chris met this girl here in Washington and hasn't been at work very much. They are talking about getting married and starting a family. He only met her after the Atlantis trip, but he claimed he was in love. Heather and I had the responsibility of making up for their absence. It was a rainy day and I was sitting in my office. I was finishing writing my speech to the nation. I was told by the President that I had to give a speech to the nation about our journey to the lost city and what new advances we were going to take in finding it. Heather walked in and sat down in front of me on my desk. I tried to ignore her because I had to get my speech finished but she started to rub my shoulders. I stopped what I was doing and looked at her.

"What are you doing?" she asked.

"Writing my speech to the nation," I answered.

"Can you take a break?"

"Yeah, for a moment anyway. Why?". Dr. Johnson walked in.

"Oh, sorry, I should have knocked."

"No, that's ok," I said.

"I just wanted to let you know that your speech will be in a few minutes," he continued.

"Yeah I know that," I said.

"But what you don't know is you have to address the press and the nation about a new mission," he continued. "The Pentagon informed the nation of a new mission but did not tell them what it was."

"So what is it, you should know," Heather asked.

"The government wants the team to investigate the end of the world.," he answered.

"Ok, let me work on it," I said. He walked out of the office.

"Let me call Chris and Krissy," Heather said. "You keep working on your speech." She walked out and I went back to writing my speech. She walked into her office and picked up the phone. She called Krissy.

"Hello," Krissy answered.

"Krissy, this is Heather."

"Oh no! Don't even think about asking me to go on one of your stupid missions. No way. I had way too many problems."

"Please Krissy, we have to do this."

"Either do it by yourselves or not at all." Krissy hung up the phone. Heather called Chris.

"Chris speaking," he answered.

"Chris, this is Heather," she said.

"Hey Heather. What's up?"

"Do you want to join us in another mission?"

"I would love to but my girlfriend said I can't if I want to stay with her."

"Please Chris we need you."

"I can't. Where are you going?"

"We are not allowed to say yet. Watch the speech tonight." She hung up the phone.

Heather walked in and informed me that neither Chris nor Krissy would go with. Dr. Johnson walked in.

"Time to leave for your speech," he said. We walked down to the conference room. This is the first time a Time Warrior gave a speech to the nation. The seal of our team was in back of the podium. Our logo was on the seal. Our logo looked like a melting metal clock.

FBI agents were waiting for me and they stood guard. The media was everywhere with cameras flashing. Heather walked with me to the podium and stood by my side. I started to think, Krissy is watching this, my parents, my grandparents, Chris, my aunts, my uncles, my teachers, friends, Heather's family and friends. An agent came up to me.

"You're on in ten seconds and by the way the nation will stop for this, no other shows are on ," he said. "5-4-3-2-1."

"Good evening," I said. "As you know my name is TJ and I am the leader of the Time Warriors. Our job is to monitor time traveling. Just over three weeks ago we got back from our second mission. Our first mission was to test time traveling. And to no surprise we had difficulties. When we got back, we became this new government team. About four weeks ago we had reason to believe that a group of criminals were going to commit the biggest crime in history. In fact, we were correct. Four criminals attempted to steal the codes of Atlantis which in fact led to the disappearance of Atlantis. In other words, time repeats itself thousands of times a day. Through our mission, we realized that there are many parallel universes, and when we leave the present, we enter the history of another universe, which is our universe at an earlier time. We still aren't sure how it works completely, but you can't change history. In other words, those criminals were meant to steal the codes and cause Atlantis to sink. I will now open the floor to questions."

"Do you have an idea as to where the remains of Atlantis may be located?"

"We have evidence that suggests its location, but I have no obligation to answer that question at this time." Heather stepped up to the mic.

"We have reason to believe it is located in the Bermuda Triangle," she said. I looked at her.

"Can you give us some of the evidence?"

"Not at this time, but it is very clear as to where the location is," she answered

"Do you have a team ready to search for it?"

"Yes, there is a company embarking on that quest," she said.

"Earlier today the FBI informed us of another mission in planning. What is your response to that?"

"As of now the mission is in planning. We have our goal but we need to work out the details."

"What is the goal of the mission and who will be involved?" Just then a FBI agent walked up and told me to close the floor.

"At this time I would like to close the floor," I said. "Thank you and good night." I walked off as the media screamed questions at me. Heather followed me. The agent told Heather and I to meet in his office in five minutes.

CHAPTER TWO

Heather and I walked into the agent's office. "Sit down," he said. At this moment I knew something was wrong. "We have a problem," he continued. "We have reports of an unidentified time machine leaving this time. The UTM left from St. Louis, Missouri and we need you two to explore the situation. You will leave for Missouri right now. The jet is waiting for you. We need you to search the location and find any information possible because we have no idea what is taking place. An officer in St. Louis will meet you at the air force base you will land at and take you directly to the scene. Good luck." Heather and I stood up and walked to the elevator. I pushed the basement button. We went into the equipment room and got our outfits. Once we were changed we left for the plane. Once the plane was in the air I kept thinking what could be so important that our mission got cancelled.

"I can't believe we have another mission," Heather said.

"I know," I responded. "And it isn't the one the government was planning."

"And we don't have Chris and Krissy," she continued.

"We'll just have to do it ourselves," I told her. I sat back in my seat and closed my eyes.

When we landed at the St. Louis air force base, the agent met us. "Follow me," he said. Even after working with the FBI for over a year, I still did not get use to them. They are so secretive. We got in a car waiting outside the base terminal and it took us deep into the city. I had been to St. Louis when I was younger and I really liked the city. I had a feeling that this time, I would not like the visit. We pulled up in front of an old building. It was dark and gloomy. The sun was setting.

"Inside is the business of the UTM we tracked. Go in, find what you can and get out as quickly as possible. Just so you know, this place is heavily guarded twenty-four hours a day." I started to walk to the door. "Where are you going," the agent asked.

"Inside," I answered.

"You can't just walk in. Use your equipment," he said. I pulled the long shot off my belt and shot it up to the roof. Heather followed. There was a guard walking around. I threw a smoke bomb and ran over to the door. I opened the door and went in. Heather followed me down the stairs. The guard that was on the roof came in the door and started shooting at us. I threw a smoke bomb up at him and he started coughing and I grabbed Heather's arm and pulled her quickly down the stairs. Then we went in the door. There was a hallway and I went in the first door. Inside there was a desk with a folder on it. I looked in the folder and found that the time machine belonged to Tyler Brooks. For some reason that name sounded familiar to me. I looked inside and saw a proposal. It looked as if though this guy was trying to get money to take over time.

165

"This guy wants to take over time," I said to Heather. She just shook her head. "But why," I asked. "What could be so important about taking over time." Jus then the door bust open and a bunch of smoke bombs flew in and filled the room with smoke. I started to cough and reached for Heather but she was gone. I scurried around the room trying to find her. Then someone hit me over the head with a metal object and I fell to the floor.

When I woke up I was chained to a wall. Tyler, I suppose was standing in front of me. He walked over and looked at me. "So, Mr. Leader, what are you going to do now?"

"Where's Heather," I asked

"Oh, she is ok," he answered.

"Let her go," I continued.

"All in due time," he said. "But first I use her as black mail. See as long as I have her, you won't be able to stop me because you will be too worried about saving her."

"What are you planning to do," I asked.

"Kill you and then take over time to control the world," he answered. "Boys, let's go." Five guys came into the room and one was holding Heather. Another brought a time machine. Then a lot of guys showed up with a lot of time machines. They all got in and left. Then Tyler threw a timed bomb at me and left. I saw the bomb was set for five minutes. I tried to free myself but it was no luck. Just then the FBI ran in and freed me. We ran out of the building and the building blew up.

"Get in touch with Chris and tell him to join me in time," I said. "I can't wait, I got to go now."

"You can't…" the agent said as I pushed the button. The wind picked up and the ground started to disintegrate. I disappeared. "You're by yourself," the agent finished.

CHAPTER THREE

When I landed in the time, I looked around. I had my time belt track Tyler and Heather. I was in a city, probably St. Louis. Just then a few flying cars flew over my head. I heard big booms in the background almost like cannons. Some people came running up the street. "What year is it," I asked.

"Leave me alone. They're after me," the man replied.

"Run," a woman yelled. I started to run with the crowd. A massive number of flying cannons flew over head. I looked up and Tyler and Heather were in the one. I realized he was going to terrorize time until he controlled it. I pulled out my long shot and shot up to the cannon behind them. I climbed up on the roof and hopped in the open window. Tyler's soldiers were inside. One walked over to me and swung at me and I ducked. I kicked him in the stomach and punched him in the face. Another one came over and tripped him and punched him. I picked up a metal bar and hit another soldier with it. I took out the last of the soldiers and then went to the driver. I knocked him out with the bar and took over the controls. I followed Tyler. Some other cannons started shooting at me so I had to swerve to miss the missiles. I slammed on the breaks and they flew past me and I shot at them blowing both cannons up. Tyler landed his and got out with Heather. They ran down the street. I landed quickly and hopped out and took off down the street with them. Heather kicked Tyler in the stomach and started to run to me. Tyler quickly turned around and grabbed Heather's arm. A couple of Tyler's thugs attacked me. One knocked me down and I took my feet and hooked them around his head and flipped him over me. Tyler ran off with Heather. I got up and ran after them and the thugs followed me. A girl ran out from an ally and grabbed my arm and pulled me in. Then she grabbed on, almost like hugging me, and jumped up to the roof of a building. She let go of me. I looked, shocked, at her.

"How did you do that," I asked.

"What do you mean," she asked.

"How did you jump like that?"

"That's my special ability."

"What special ability?"

"Where are you from?" I walked over to the edge of the building and looked down. The thugs were down there looking for me.

"Jump," she said.

"Are you nuts?"

"Just jump. Trust me."

"Trust you, I just met you." She pushed me off the edge of the building and I stopped in mid-air. She pulled me back up on the roof. "What the hell is going on," I asked. "What year is it?"

"5194." I looked at her. "Now do you trust me?"

"Yeah, I guess."

"Good, you can help me."

"With what?"

"I am trying to get my boyfriend back from these weird people. Those guys that were chasing you took him."

"Well, that's good, cause I am trying to get my girlfriend back from them too." She walked off the edge of the building and started walking down the air like it was steps.

"Well, don't just stand there, let's go." I closed my eyes and stepped off the building. I started to walk down the air and it felt like steps. I opened my eyes and finished walking down them.

"This place is too weird. I don't like it." I followed her down the street. When we got to the end of the block, which was really long, she stopped.

"This is where they are."

"How do you know that?"

"I have special abilities, remember." I just smiled and couldn't believe what I was seeing and hearing. She walked into the building and I followed. The door closed behind us and a bunch of thugs jumped out. They surrounded us. I thought to myself, "Triton I could really use your help now." Just then a bubble of water appeared next to me and Triton appeared.

"Hey, what's up," he said. "You called." The thugs just looked at him. He made a bunch of surf boards appear and threw them to the thugs. "Get ready to surf." He floated into the air and his eyes lit up. A wave appeared behind him and he threw his arms forward and it washed the thugs away. He disappeared. I walked up the steps to a closed door and stood there listening.

"You are so pathetic," Tyler said. "You think your boyfriend will save you. You don't realize how powerful I am. You can call me the Master of Time because I know that there are parallel universes and I know how to use them."

"How do you know this," Heather asked.

"You would never imagine the connections I have. Watch this." He picked up a walkie talkie. "Kelly, can you hear me?"

"I hear you," a girl's voice answered.

"Get your boyfriend on the phone," Tyler said.

"Yeah," a guy's voice answered.

"Do you know this voice," Tyler asked Heather.

"That's Chris," she screamed. "Chris!!!" He threw her down on the ground and she cracked her head on the floor.

"Chris," Tyler said. "tell me what I need to know about the dinosaurs."

"Just be careful," Chris answered, "be cautious and don't make any sudden movements."

"Thanks Chris," Tyler said.

"No problem," Chris said.

I was wondering why Chris would help Tyler. I ran in the room and Tyler turned around. I went to grab Heather but he grabbed on to her and snapped his fingers and a time machine appeared. He took Heather inside. I tried to jump head first inside but he close the door and I ran my head into the door. The machine started to spin and lifted into the air. I pressed the button on my belt and the wind picked up and the ground started to disintegrate and I disappeared into a tunnel of darkness. I saw the machine in front of me and I tried to catch up with it. I saw the light at the end of the tunnel. The machine shot out into space and then I did. The machine and I just floated in the air. I looked in the window and Tyler waved to me.

"Don't wave to me," I said. "I'm right on your tail." He shook his head no. He shot a bubble out of the machine and it surrounded me. The Earth started to spin counter clock wise and then the machine fell into the Earth and I just floated there. I took out my laser and shot the bubble. It burst and I fell toward the Earth. The Earth started to spin. "That's not good," I said. I started to breathe heavily. I fell into the atmosphere as the Earth was spinning. I stopped falling right above the surface and when the Earth was done spinning I landed. "Man, the asshole really does know how to control time," I said. I looked around and I saw I was back in the present day, St. Louis. I used my belt to warp back to Washington.

CHAPTER FOUR

I walked right up and into my office. On the way to my office some FBI agents tried to talk to me but I just ignore them. I went on my computer and typed in Tyler Brooks. The screen came up and gave me his information.

TYLER BROOKS

BORN: 1983

CITY BORN: ST. LOUIS

PARENTS: RICHARD AND JEAN BROOKS

SIBLINGS: 2; SISTER KELLY; BROTHER DAVID

OCCUPATION: UNKNOWN

EDUCATION: HARVARD; DOCTORATE DEGREE IN ENGINEERING

I sat back in my chair and started to ponder everything I had just learned about him. He is one year older than me but yet he completed a doctorate degree which means he was advanced in school. So he must be extremely smart. But he must have known that he wanted to take over time because he has a degree in engineering which is probably the field to have under your belt for time traveling. I still think this name sounds familiar.

Then I started to think about his family. "That's it," I screamed. His sister is Chris' girlfriend. That's why Chris is giving him information and Chris doesn't realize he's using the information against us. I picked up the phone and called Chris. Kelly answered.

"Kelly, this is TJ, get me Chris," I said.

"No, you can't talk to him," she said. She hung up the phone. I figured she wouldn't want me to talk to him because I would tell him that Tyler is using the information to take over time. An FBI agent walked into my office.

"So how are things going," he asked. "Where's Heather?"

"Ha," I said, "things are terrible. We went to St. Louis and we found out that this guy, Tyler Brooks, was going to master time and use it against society to control the world. He and his thugs kidnapped Heather and led me into the future to 5194 where I met up with this freak. She was this teenage girl who possessed these bizarre powers. She helped me try to get Heather back. Oh yeah, they had flying cars. We went to the place the thugs were and were outnumbered. I asked for Triton's help and he came and helped me. Then I heard Tyler talking to Chris about going to the time of the dinosaurs. Tyler and Heather disappeared into time and I followed but he trapped me and sent me back here. I tried to call Chris but Kelly wouldn't let me talk to him. I looked up Tyler's file and found out that he is one year older than me, Kelly's brother, and has a degree in engineering. I found out that Chris is helping Tyler because he is Kelly's brother and he doesn't realize that Tyler is using the info against us."

"What are you going to do," the agent asked.

"I'm going back to the dinosaurs and I am going to catch him. And when I do... well never mind."

"I'll address the nation because the President thinks they are overly concerned that you didn't address the next mission. And since you are going back, I make the speech."

"But first, I'm going to Chris' house," I said.

Meanwhile in Northampton, my parents were watching TV. Breaking news flashed across the screen. "Good afternoon, and welcome to a NTV news special report," Paul McDoughry said. "Last night the leader of the Time Warriors addressed the nation. During his speech he avoided questions about the next mission. However, right now we have a FBI agent about to address the nation. Let's go live to Washington, D.C." The screen switched to the FBI building. The agent walked out to the mic. "Good afternoon. Less than twenty-four hours ago, the leader of the Time Warriors addressed the nation about some issues. However, he left out the next mission. The mission was being planned for the team to go into the future and investigate the end of the world. TJ was going to tell you that last night. The reason he didn't was because another mission came up. During his speech last night a UTM, unidentified time machine, left this time period. We had reason to believe this was criminal activity. The team left from the meeting for St. Louis last night and found out that indeed it was criminal activity. They found out that a criminal was planning to master time and control the world. However, in the process of finding this out they were attacked. Heather has been kidnapped. TJ is following the group, by himself, through time. As we speak the President is on the phone with other countries around the world trying to get the best advice because this is a world problem. For now, TJ will continue to pursue the criminals by himself. Good night and God bless." The agent walked away.

I walked up to Chris apartment in Washington, D.C. and knocked on the door. I looked around to make sure there was nobody watching me. Kelly opened the door and I pushed in as she tried to close the door. Some thugs jumped down from the roof. I punched one and kicked another. One swung at me and I ducked under it and punched him in the stomach. I kicked back and kicked the one behind me in the stomach. I took a hold of the two aside of me by the heads and cracked them together. By this time Kelly had closed the door and locked it. I stood there banging on the door. It wasn't working so I figured instead of wasting this much time I could be chasing Tyler through time. I pressed my belt. A black screen appeared before my eyes and asked me where I wanted to go. "St. Louis, Missouri; dinosaur period," I said.

"Access denied," the computer said back.

"What do you mean access denied, you can't do that," I said. "St. Louis, Missouri; dinosaur period."

"Access denied."

"AAAAHHHH," I screamed. "He can't do this to me!!!!" Everyone stopped and looked at me. "This is personal," I screamed at the people around me. "He started a personal war. This is as personal as it gets. Wait till' I get my hands on him. I'll strangle him. He really does know how to control time and he is only getting stronger." Everyone was still staring. "What are you looking at!!!! There is nothing to see here. Move on!!" I started jumping up and down kicking things. The people hurried off.

At the White House a lot of activity was happening. The President was busy talking to the leaders of other countries about what to do. They had extra guards around because they feared Tyler would go after the President.

CHAPTER FIVE

I stood there on the sidewalk trying to figure out what to do. I took a cab back to my office. As I was walking to the elevator an FBI agent came up to me.

"Can I help in anyway," the agent asked me.

"Do we have another way of getting back in time," I asked.

"I don't know. You have to ask Dr. Johnson. Why?"

"Tyler found a way to control my traveling device and it won't let me have access." I walked into the elevator and pushed the basement button. When I got to the lab, Dr. Johnson was sitting there. "Make yourself useful," I said. "Find me a way to travel."

"Nice to see you too," he responded as he got up from where he was sitting. "Why, what is wrong with your device?"

"Tyler found a way to control it and I can't access it."

"Well, there is a way but it hasn't been tested."

"I don't care. Let me try it."

"Hold on, let me try to fix your device." He looked at it and turned some knobs.

"Try it." I took it from him and pushed the button. The black screen appeared and asked me where I wanted to go.

"Find Tyler Brooks."

"Access allowed," it said as the wind picked up and the ground started to disintegrate. The black hole formed and I flew down into it. I flew through the tunnel and out into space. The Earth started to spin counter-clock wise. When the Earth stopped I flew toward it and entered the atmosphere. As I approached the surface I saw time machines. When I landed I looked around and the ground started to shake. Being here before I knew immediately that it was the dinosaur we met first. I looked around and to my right I saw the trees moving. It came flying out into the field and headed toward me. I took off running. It followed me, and I wasn't able to outrun it. I ran toward the trees and climbed up one. It got over to the tree and I froze. It was looking over at me and sniffing. It left and I climbed down. I looked around and saw no signs of Tyler except the time machines. I walked through the woods and got to a cliff. When I looked down I saw Tyler and Heather on the cliff below so I laid down on the ground. Heather looked up and saw me and I signaled her to be quiet.

"So Heather, I heard you have experience jumping off cliffs," Tyler said.

"Yeah, so," Heather replied.

"So, you won't mind jumping down there."

"No way, there's no water."

"That's the point."

"I'll die."

"But it's a worthy cause. For me anyway." He drug her by the arm out to the edge of the cliff they were on. He was getting ready to throw her off the cliff so I jumped down. He turned around and looked at me. I went to punch him but he ducked and flipped me over his back. I turned around and kicked him in the chest and he fell backwards. He got up and ran at me and I moved. He almost fell off the edge. He turned around and pushed me into a rock and I hit my head. I pretended to be knocked out. Heather jumped on his back and started to hit him in the head. He grabbed her by the neck and threw her on the ground. I got up and kicked him in the face, he fell over, and I grabbed Heather by the arm and ran.

"On three, push your button," I said. "One, two three." We both pushed our buttons and the wind picked up and the ground disintegrated. We flew down the tunnel and out into space. I programmed in the present day.

"Get in the machines," Tyler screamed at his thugs. "And catch them." They climbed in their time machines and took off. Heather and I were floating in space and the Earth started to spin clockwise. Tyler was there and the Earth stopped spinning. Tyler shot a bubble at it and caused it to start spinning again.

"What's he doing," Heather asked.

"Changing time," I answered. We started to fall into the Earth.

CHAPTER SIX

When the Earth stopped spinning and we landed on the surface it was dark. I was squinting to try to figure out where we were. Heather walked over and held on to my arm. There was no sign of anyone around. I saw structures of some sort. I couldn't tell if they were buildings or not. I started to walk and Heather followed still holding on to my arm. I kept an eye out for Tyler. Once I took notice to the temperature I realized it was really cold. I heard something more horrible than I had ever heard before. It sounded like an animal screeching. I looked around and saw two eyes glowing green in the dark. Heather squeezed my arm harder.

"Wha-what's that," she asked.

"I don't know, but it doesn't look friendly." We started to back up and it stepped out into view. It was a huge, alien-looking creature. It had a black body. It's head was like a cat but really evil looking. It opened it's mouth and I saw huge, sharp teeth. Then it growled and started swinging it's arms with huge claws at us.

"Where are we," Heather asked.

"Apparently Earth in a far off future."

"What do we do," she asked. I pulled away from her and walked towards it.

"TJ, be careful," Heather cried. The creature stood up on its legs and it was about the size of me in height but much bigger in mass. It screamed a nail on a chalkboard cry and I held my ears. It swung its arm at me and cut my shoulder. I grabbed my shoulder with the blood pouring on to my hand.

"Run," I yelled to Heather. As I started to turn away from the creature I saw a mass of them flying from all directions.

"Oh, my God," Heather cried. "What do we do?"

"Hit the button," I said. We both pushed it and the black screen appeared.

"St. Louis, present day," Heather said.

"Access denied," it replied.

"St. Louis, present day," I screamed.

"Access denied," it replied.

"No," I screamed! "He can't do this." I grabbed Heather's arm and started to run. The creatures were swooping down at us but we ducked and dodged them. Heather was screaming as we were running and my shoulder kept bleeding. The cut was deep and I knew I had to close it soon. I saw light coming from the horizon and it quickly covered the land. The creatures dove down. Heather and I fell and braced for the attack. We felt no attack. I opened my eyes and saw they were gone. Standing there were to figures in the darkness with crystals in their hands. I stood up and then Heather did. "Who are you," I asked. They were standing a good distance away that I couldn't see them.

"My name is TJ and this is Heather," a voice replied. I walked towards them and saw that they were us.

"Oh my God," Heather exclaimed. "That's us." I couldn't believe that we were staring at us, but we didn't have time to find out why or how.

"So why did those creatures disappear," I asked.

"These crystals are designed to scare them," TJ replied. "Follow me," he said, "We've been expecting you." He walked away.

"You have," I said. Heather and I followed them. He led us through the ruins of the city or what use to be a city. We headed toward the mountains. "What city is this," I asked.

"St. Louis," TJ replied.

"What happened to it," Heather asked.

"I'll show you," he answered. He continued to lead us and when we got to the mountains he stopped. He held up the crystal and a door opened in the mountain. We walked inside. The door closed behind us and I looked around. It was dark so I couldn't see anything. "Sit," he said as chairs came up behind us. Heather looked at me and we sat down. He clapped his hands and a vision appeared in front of us. "This is my world," he said.

A movie started. "From the beginning of time, the Earth has been a haven for disaster. From extraterrestrial objects like comets to wars and plagues. Massive extinctions have occurred but not to the extent of the one that wiped out humans." I looked at Heather. The screen was showing massive destruction. "Humans began to become too smart and powerful for Mother Earth to hold them. One man became the Master of Time and only two young people could stand in his way of becoming ruler and destructor of the world. However those two people were not powerful enough and perished in the process. The Master of Time overcame them in a long, gruesome, painful battle. The two great warriors battled to the death and the Master of Time took over and destroyed the world. But because the two warriors knew how to control parallel worlds they survived in another dimension. That dimension combined all of history with the future the Earth never saw. The Master of Time unlocked a spell of evil on the planet wiping out every human and set loose an army of evil cat-like aliens. He used weapons of mass destruction to destroy every city, contaminate all the water, and make the Earth a haunted wasteland. On the other hand, the two great warriors set up a collection of the past, present, and future in a mountain chain, protected from the evil. This is the only remains of the planet known as Earth.

CHAPTER SEVEN

The movie stopped and I looked at Heather, she was already looking at me. "I guess you two have a lot of questions, but before I answer them, let me show you." He got up and walked away and we followed. He led us deep into the mountain and clapped. Lights came on and the pyramids of Egypt stood before us.

"Wow," Heather said.

"That's unbelievable," I added. He walked into the next room and once again clapped. The lights came on revealing the Walls of Babylon and the Statue of Zeus. The next room revealed a field of dinosaurs running and living as if it was their time period. There were thousands of rooms like that with the Statue of Liberty, Great Wall of China, Niagara Falls, the list goes on.

"The reason I knew you were coming," he said as the girl walked up to him. "Is because we are you, and we did this already. You two are the great warriors the story talked about. I know your fate, and now you do to. You will die in a long, painful, gruesome battle but you will live on in this dimension. The Master of Time is undefeatable but once he kills you, you will create this masterpiece of time. The world will be destroyed in front of your eyes and you will have a limited time to save the most precious elements of time. A mountain range will form for you right by

St. Louis and the mountains will be hollow." There was a flash of light and we were back

in our offices in the present day.

"That was weird," Heather said.

"Yeah, I know," I said.

"So we won't win," she said.

"I guess not." There was silence. "I wish they would of told us what his master

plan was."

"They wanted to leave it interesting," she answered.

"I want to know where Chris and Krissy fit into this picture," I said. Just then

Dr. Johnson walked in.

"We have a problem," he started.

"Oh boy, here we go again," I said.

"He went after the President and his family," Dr. Johnson continued.

"Who," Heather asked

"Tyler," Dr. Johnson answered.

"Let's go," I said. We made our way to the basement and grabbed the usual

equipment. We hopped on the motorcycles and rode to the White House. When we got

to the front gate there were FBI agents there.

"Stop," one agent said as he signaled for us to stop. We slowed down.

"Time Warrior business," I said.

"You don't belong here," he answered. "You investigate time."

"The person that did this is trying to become the master of time," Heather said.

"How do you know who did this," he asked.

"There is a guy trying to master time, actually he already did, but he wants to take over the world. It kind of makes sense," I replied.

"Let them through," another agent yelled. "The president's orders." They opened the gate and we drove through. When we got in front of the White House I looked around to make sure none of Tyler's thugs were still there. We got off the bikes and went in. The President greeted us.

"My son has been kidnapped by that evil mastermind," he said.

"Don't worry sir, we'll get him back," I comforted the President.

"He left you this," the President said. "That's all I found." He handed me the piece of paper. I opened it and read it.

Dear Time Warriors,

I surely fooled you this time. You never expected me to kidnap the president's son. The reason you didn't know, is because I didn't know. I didn't expect for Heather to get loose, but she did and so I had to move to plan B. Don't worry, I won't hurt him too bad. But then it won't matter because no one's going to live to see him returned to the first family. But first the world is going to watch their new heroes die. I am heading to a place you have been in your travels. The

World of Water is my destination. I am dropping by to say hello to Poseidon.

I put the letter down and looked at Heather. "He's going after Triton," I said.

"Let's go," she cried.

"Good luck," the President said. We pushed the buttons on our belts and programmed in Atlantis. The floor disintegrated around us and we flew down the tunnel of darkness. We shot out into space and the Earth started to spin counter-clockwise. When it stopped we fell to the surface and sure enough we were in Atlantis. Tyler's thugs met us inside the gate. He had some girls there too. A couple of girls went after Heather. She kicked them in the stomach and knocked them to the ground. Some of the guys ran at me and I flipped them over me and onto the ground. More came running and we were being surrounded. Triton floated down from the sky.

"Man, am I glad to see you," I said. His eyes lit up and he threw his arms back. A wave appeared in back of his arms. He thrusted them forward and washed the thugs away.

"So, what brings you here," Triton asked.

"There is this guy from our time that is trying to master time and he kidnapped our leader's son. He left us a note that he was going to visit the World of Water, which I automatically knew this was it," I answered.

"I haven't seen him," Triton continued. "How are you?" He looked at Heather.

"Just fine," she answered, "and you?"

"Wonderful," he answered.

CHAPTER EIGHT

Triton led us down into his home underground. "So, what's been happening," he asked.

"Well we're after this mad man who is trying to become the Master of Time," I answered.

"Yeah," Heather said. "And we found out that he will win."

"So what is he doing here," Triton asked.

"That's what we're trying to figure out," Heather replied.

"You never know what is going on," Triton continued. "Last time the criminals stole the Codes of Atlantis before you figured out that what they were after."

"That's it," I said. "He knows we're going to collect pieces of time and he wants to take the Codes before we do."

"I have a way to warp up to my father's temple," Triton said. "Being a god has its avantages." He held on to our arms and seconds later we were standing in the entrance of Poseidon's temple. I looked at Heather and she shook a little.

"Are you alright," I asked Heather.

"Yeah, this place just gives me the creeps," she answered. We walked down the hall and into the main chamber. I heard a kid screaming and realized it was Josh, the president's son. I ran through the hall leading out of the chamber while Triton and

Heather stood there. I ran down the cave steps to the cave below the temple where the codes are stored. When I came to a "Y" in the passage ways I stopped and listened. A cold breeze went by. Then I saw a few of Tyler's thugs walking toward me. I turned around and there were more. I ran down the branch off that had no thugs. This led me back upstairs in the temple. I heard the thugs running up the steps after me. I saw some weapons on the wall and walked over to them. Then I heard Triton's voice in my subconscious. "Don't touch anything or you will awaken the guardians of the temple." I thought to myself that I beat them before, I'll beat them again. I grabbed a staff from the wall. Suddenly, behind me, water dripped from the ceiling. It formed puddles and the puddles turned into water warriors. I grabbed some more weapons and started throwing them to the thugs. More and more water warriors were forming. The water warriors looked at me and I pointed to the thugs, which had all the weapons and I had none. I moved out of the way and the warriors attacked the thugs. I ran back to the main chamber where Triton and Heather were fighting off a few thugs. I ran in and helped. Once we had knocked all of the thugs out, Tyler stood in front of us. He threw a smoke bomb down and disappeared.

"Did he get the codes," Heather asked.

"No," Triton said. "My father would have destroyed the temple." He led us out of the temple. Then he warped us back to his home. "You're welcome to stay the night," he said. "It is pretty late." I looked at his clock made out of water and it was ten o'clock.

"We'll stay for the night," I said. "But we leave early in the morning and try to figure out where Tyler is going next."

"Well," Triton said. "I'm going to bed, you know where the guest room is and how to get around the city if you need to, good night."

"Let's go sit out by one of the buildings that makes music," Heather said. I agreed and we walked down the hallway and climbed up the ladder. We walked down the street and found a place of green grass, with sparkling water in the creek, the stars shining brightly above, and the music playing from the wind hitting the buildings near by. We sat there staring at the sky. There were no lights from the city, so you could see the milky way and other galaxies.

"Why should we fight if we are going to lose," Heather asked.

"Because I have a feeling that Tyler set that little scenario in the future up to make us give up," I answered. "See I think he is just trying to scare us out of the fight." We heard some noise coming from across the creek. We got up and ran behind the trees that were nearby. Tyler was on the other side of the creek with Josh. Josh went down and got a handful of water to drink.

"You'll never get away with this," Josh said after taking a drink. "The great Time Warriors will stop you."

"Ha," Tyler laughed. "So that's what your daddy calls them. Great Time Warriors, ha, ha, ha." He walked over and grabbed Josh's short blonde hair. "No one will stop me, not even the great Time Warriors." He threw Josh into the creek and Josh hit his head on a rock. Tyler walked away laughing and saying "great Time Warriors". Two

191

thugs came into view and picked Josh up and carried him away. I ran toward them and splashed through the creek. When I got half way through the creek Tyler jumped out from behind the trees on and shot a glowing bullet at me. The bullet opened up and formed an invisible wall between me and him. I stood there banging on the wall. It shimmered as I touched it.

"Hey," I screamed. "You think you'll get away with this, but you won't. We're on to you. We'll get you."

"Ha," he replied. "You're even funnier than the kid. You are wrong. You are not on to me. This war is only beginning, this now is kid stuff. You have no idea how in depth this war is. You don't even know half of what is going to happen. Let the games begin." He hopped in the time machine the thugs brought out for him. They put Josh in too and it disappeared. I could hear him from the time portal saying "This is the beginning. Let the games begin."

CHAPTER NINE

"Good evening," the President said. He was about to make an address to the

nation. "Let me start by saying, I hope all is well. I also want to say my prayers go out to

the family members of the great warriors. The great warriors are our life savers, they are

the ones our future counts on. They are, from what I understand, about to engage in a

massive battle of technology. I was told by them that they will either win or die in the

process of trying. Next I will let the nation know that my son has been kidnapped by the

Master of Time. So this is more personal than I would have liked it to be. Now, what am

I doing about it? I have contacted the United Nations and asked them to join in the battle

against this evil. Some Americans have been writing to me and asking what they can do

to help. My answer to them is, pray. This is a test for the world, not just Americans. If

this Master of Time succeeds there will be nothing left of the Earth. I have prepared our

nation's forces to protect us here in the present if he should unleash evil on us. But I am

not too concerned about that yet. Right now he is more concerned with destroying the

great warriors. He has unimaginable power and this is almost impossible for the warriors

to win. I tell you this so you know that we have little chance of winning this war. A question you may have is, why are we not sending our forces to help? The answer, our forces will not make a difference. He is too powerful and it is easier to have two people sneak in and attack than a whole army. Our country will go on, we will continue our everyday lives. Don't let him get to us. Think about the two brave warriors out there somewhere in time fighting him. He is not getting to them, so let's not let him get to us. I will suggest however, that you spend time with your family and especially your younger children. Make them feel safe and help them understand that we are doing all we can do. But most of all, keep praying for our warriors. Good night and God bless." He walked out of the conference room.

"So that was the President's address to the nation about the Master of Time. Thank you for watching KWZ news, I'm James Book." My mom turned off the TV and walked into the kitchen. She got a soda from the refrigerator. She sat down at the table and just stared out the window. My dad walked in the house, he was just getting home from the market.

CHAPTER TEN

Chris walked into his apartment. Kelly was sitting on the sofa. "Hey Chris," Kelly said. Chris just walked to the kitchen and grabbed a soda. "What's the matter," Kelly asked.

"My friends are the two warriors the President talked about and they're in trouble."

"Yeah, so do what the President said, pray."

"But I could be out there helping them just like I used to."

"Chris, I have to tell you something. I can trust you right."

"Yes, of course, tell me what you need to."

"Ever since I could remember, my older brother was playing games, writing stories, and talking about world domination. He kept telling me, wait and see. I never knew what he was talking about. Then, when you and your friends did the impossible thing of time traveling, he became interested in it. He studied all the theories, books, fiction, anything that had to do with time traveling. He started a lab in an old warehouse with a huge group of others willing to help. He created a way to control time and master it. He kept talking about how he had a plan to take over the world, but he kept saying he would not fail like Napoleon and Khan. He said he was going to take it over showing no mercy. And then, he showed me his plans."

"So you're telling me that he used me to fight my friends," Chris said shocked.

"I am telling you that the only reason I went out with you is because it is part of his plan."

"Wait, all this time I have been hurting my friends and I didn't even know it."

"Yeah, they called thousands of times trying to get you to help, but I kept telling them you wanted nothing to do with them. Chris you promised, now you have to help me and Tyler. You'll get to live when he wins and you can be an advisor to him when he rules the world. What do you say?"

"No way. If my friends die, I die. Now if I get Krissy to help, we might have a chance of defeating him."

"No you don't have a chance. He created evil cat-like monsters that he is going to unleash against the world. He has weapons that will play games with your friends that they will never figure out how to beat. He has weapons of mass destruction ready and aiming at every city in the world."

"Good, then there is no time to loose." He ran out of the apartment and to the Time Warrior offices. He got in elevator and went to the basement. He went to the equipment room and changed into his outfit. Then he grabbed the equipment that he needed. "Now, I talk to Krissy." He took one of the motorcycles and headed to downtown Washington, where Krissy lived.

Meanwhile, Kelly called Tyler. "Tyler's office," a secretary answered.

"This is Kelly," she said. "Is Tyler there?"

"No, he isn't."

"Ok, thank you." Kelly put he phone down. She thought about how to help Tyler. Then she remembered Chris said he was going to get Krissy. She walked over to the fireplace and pressed the button. It turned around revealing a hidden lab. Nick was working on a new chemical. "Let's go," Kelly said to Nick. "We need to stop Chris and Krissy before they get to their friends."

"But I need to help Tyler," Nick said.

"I'll send Jessy to help him," Kelly continued. She walked over to the cage where one of the cat-like aliens was. "Your time is coming. What is Tyler calling them?"

"K.A.T.S.," Nick answered. "Because they have Killer Anibotic Thriving Syndrome. In other words, they're animals that thrive to kill."

"Nice," Kelly said. "I'm sure our great warriors will love to meet them."

Chris pulled up in front of Krissy's house. He got off the bike and walked to the door. He knocked on the door. Krissy answered the door.

"Hey Krissy," Chris said as she opened the door. When Krissy saw who it was she slammed the door in his face. Chris knocked again. Krissy didn't answer so he opened the door. "Krissy, you forgot to lock it."

"Get out. I don't want to talk to you," she yelled.

"Krissy you don't mean that."

"Yes I do. Get out."

"But didn't you see the president's address to the nation?"

"Yeah, so."

"So, TJ and Heather need our help."

"No way am I going to help them. I had enough trouble in the past."

"But if we don't help them, they'll die. And if they die, we die."

"Really?"

"Yeah, if we don't stop this guy, he'll kill us all."

"But still, I was just a problem in the past, I never really helped."

"Yeah, that' true, but now is your chance."

"No, I still will not help."

"Fine, I am not wasting my time anymore. I need to be out there helping them. But if we loose and you didn't help us, the world will be destroyed and you will feel guilty because you could have been the missing link. Then you'll be destroyed with the world all because you were too selfish. Goodbye." He walked out of the house and slammed the door. Krissy looked out the window.

"I think I made the right decision," she said to herself but she was doubting it in her heart.

CHAPTER ELEVEN

"So where do we go," Heather asked.

"I don't know," I answered. We were still in Atlantis. Then I saw a few thugs getting ready to leave. "When they leave we'll follow them through the warp zone." They got in the machines and the machines disappeared. I looked at Heather and nodded and we pressed the buttons. The ground disintegrated and we flew down the tunnel after the machines. "Faster," I yelled to Heather. "We have to move faster if we want to catch them." She looked at me with a stare that said I don't know how to go faster. "Click the heels of your boots, they have rocket boosters," I said. We clicked the heels together and fire shot out of them and we flew faster toward them. The speed was too much, I was getting sick. We shot out into space and the Earth spun counter-clockwise. We stopped there by re-clicking our heels. The machines just floated there. The machine doors opened and two thugs jumped out. They flew over to us. I kicked the one in the stomach. "I didn't know we could fight in the warp zone," I said to Heather. Heather slapped the other thug across the face and punched him in the stomach. The Earth stopped spinning and the thugs hurried back to the machines. The machines started to fall toward the Earth and then we did too. The machine door opened again and they shot out a bubble. It captured Heather. "Heather," I yelled. The thug laughed knowing I wouldn't continued to follow them. But I flew up to Heather and pulled out the laser and blasted the bubble. Then we clicked our heel and flew down toward the Earth.

"TJ, turn off the boosters," Heather yelled. "Or else we'll cause too much friction in the atmosphere and we'll burn up."

"Yeah," I said. "But if we turn them off we won't catch them because they'll make the Earth spin."

"Turn them off."

"No!"

"Then go alone!"

"Fine, I will!" She turned off her boosters and stopped flying. She floated there.

"AAAAHHHH!" I screamed as I clicked off the boosters and floated up to her. I pulled out my tracking device and threw it down at the Earth. "This will track the time period they're in."

Meanwhile back in Washington, Chris was still sitting outside Krissy's house. Kelly and Nick warped onto Krissy's roof. "Are the KATS ready," Kelly asked Nick.

"Yeah," he answered

"Good, let's get rid of these two so they can't help the others." Nick pressed a button on his watch and a flock of KATS came flying in. Chris looked up when he heard screeching.

"Oh my God. What the hell is that?" he screamed. Krissy was still looking out the window and saw them. She grabbed two knives and ran outside.

"Here," Krissy yelled to Chris as she threw him a knife.

"Ha," Kelly said. Krissy and Chris looked up at them. "You're going to try to kill the KATS with knives." Kelly started laughing. "The only thing that harms them is the chemical these crystals emit. It's unfortunate for you that only four people on this planet hold these crystals." The KATS dove down at Chris and Krissy. Chris cut one with the knife but it healed immediately.

"We have to get the crystals," he yelled to Krissy.

"Alright, you distract the KATS and I'll get the crystals," Krissy replied. Krissy ran in the house and up the stairs. She opened the door to the attic and ran up those stairs. Chris was still outside fighting off the KATS by slashing them. Krissy opened the window in the roof and climbed out onto the roof. Nick ran over at her and she punched him in the face and then in the stomach. He pulled out the crystal to break it but she kicked it out of his hand and it flew off the roof. Chris saw it falling and dove over and caught it. A group of kats came diving at Chris and he closed his eyes as he held the crystal up. They screeched and flew away. He opened his eyes.

"Get the other one," Chris yelled to Krissy. Nick jumped down. Chris got up and ran over and knocked him down. He started punching him. Krissy ran after Kelly as Kelly tried to jump off the roof. Krissy caught her and threw her down on the roof. Krissy ran over and Kelly kicked her in the face. Krissy fell backwards.

201

"Get the crystal back," Kelly screamed to Nick. Nick threw Chris off of him and got up. He punched Chris in the head and Chris fell. He grabbed the crystal. Kelly kicked Krissy in the back as she was standing up and Krissy fell. "Let's go," Kelly said to Nick. They hit the buttons on their watches and disappeared. Chris got up and Krissy was coming outside.

"If that was a sign of what is to come," Chris said. "We will have no problem."

"Are you crazy," Krissy said as she laughed. "That is probably the easy stuff. But you can count me in. After all we are a team aren't we?"

Back in the warp zone, Heather and I were still floating there. I was thinking what to do next. The tracking device on my belt went off and I looked at it. It told me that the thugs went to ancient Egypt. I told Heather and we programmed it into our time devices. The Earth started to spin counter-clockwise again. When it stopped we floated down to the surface. I looked around and saw a pyramid. "Over there," I said to Heather as I pointed. "In the Pyramid." We started to walk over to the pyramid. When we got to the entrance there were guards. "Let's go around back."

"Here we go sneaking around again," Heather said. We walked around back and I pulled out my laser and cut a block out of the pyramid. I boosted Heather up and she climbed through. Then I boosted myself up and slipped through. I reached down and pulled the block back into place. Inside it was dim, the only light was candles. I heard water dripping. "There are probably more guards," Heather said.

"Yeah, and your point," I replied. She just shook her head. I stopped and

202

listened and heard Josh's voice coming from down a passageway. I waved for Heather to follow me.

CHAPTER TWELVE

We walked down the passageway and followed Josh's voice. I could hear him yelling for help. When we got down into the main chamber we ducked down behind some barrels. I looked and saw Josh lying on a table. He was chained to the table. There were Egyptians around him chanting something. Then I saw Tyler.

"Sacrifice him," Tyler was yelling, "to the Gods. Give him to the Gods. Make the Gods happy. They'll reward you with better crops." Then I saw an Egyptian walk in. He was completely covered and was carrying an ax. I jumped out and the Egyptians turned around. I started fighting them. Heather ran out and over to Josh. She started to pull on the chains trying to get him loose. She ran over and kicked the guy with the ax in the stomach. She grabbed the ax and ran back to Josh. She lifted the ax and aimed at the chain.

"Watch out," Josh yelled. Heather turned around and Tyler punched her in the face and she fell backwards. Tyler grabbed the ax and was going to use it on Heather. He lifted it up. I ran over and grabbed it from behind him and pulled it out of his hands. I took the ax and threw it in the pool of water nearby. He turned around and punched me in the face. I stumbled backwards.

"Awaken the Gods," Tyler was yelling to the Egyptians. "Summon their armies." The Egyptians ran out of the room with a book, chanting something. "See you later," Tyler said as he pressed his watch and disappeared. I helped Heather up and then grabbed an ax from the wall and cut the chains off Josh. Heather went over to him to make sure he was ok.

"We have to go," I said. "We'll chat later."

"What's the rush," Heather asked.

"They're going to summon the armies of the Gods." I grabbed her arm and she grabbed Josh's arm. We ran out of the main chamber. Josh couldn't run because his ankles were soar from the chains so I picked him up and carried him. I pushed the block out of the back of the pyramid and we climbed out. When we got outside I saw the kingdom nearby. Then I saw, standing in front of us, a lot of Egyptians led by the Queen.

"Queen Cleopatra, awaken the armies," the Egyptians were yelling. She started chanting something. Then out of the sand came a massive army of creatures.

"That's not good," Heather said. "I don't think they are treating us like royalty."

"I hope this isn't how they treat royalty," I said. The army started to march toward us.

"Didn't the Greeks and Egyptians ever fight," Heather asked.

"Probably," I said. "Why?"

"Triton would be helpful now," she continued. Then I saw the leader of the creatures appear in front of the army. I felt a drop of water on my arm. I looked and there were puddles forming around us. Triton appeared in front of us and a water army appeared behind him.

"Get ready," Triton yelled to his army of water warriors. "Attack!!!" They ran toward the Egyptian army. Before I knew it there was water and sand flying everywhere. The water army was wiping out the sand army. Triton ran to the leader of the Egyptian army and fought him. He floated into the air and threw his arms back. He created a massive wave in back of him. "Let's go surfing," he said. He threw his arms forward and the wave wiped out the leader and the last of the army. He turned around and waved to us and then disappeared.

"Let's get Josh home," I said. "Heather hold his one arm and I'll hold his other."

"Are you sure this is going to work," Heather asked.

"I don't know let's see," I answered. We pressed our belts and programmed in Washington, D.C. present day. The ground disintegrated and we flew down the tunnel and shot out into space. The Earth spun clockwise and when it stopped we floated to the surface. We landed in front of the White House and took Josh inside. The First Lady ran over and embraced Josh in her arms.

"Thank you," the President said.

"No problem," I replied. "That's our job." I looked at Heather and signaled to get ready to leave.

"Good luck," the president said.

"Let the games begin," I said to Heather.

"Great," she replied.

"It is now just beginning," I said as we pushed the buttons and headed into the warp zone.

CHAPTER THIRTEEN

When we got into space I shot my tracking device down at the Earth. "Find Tyler," I said. It flew toward the Earth. I looked at Heather and said, "Now we wait until it finds Tyler."

Meanwhile back in the present, Chris and Krissy got to the offices and Chris started to wonder how he could possibly find us. Chris went into my office and sat down. He turned on my computer. Then he looked through history and found that I had looked up Tyler. He looked through the program lists to see what it offered. He could not find anyway of tracking us. Krissy ran downstairs to Dr. Johnson.

"How do we find them," she asked him.

"Who," he asked.

"TJ and Heather," she replied. "Who do you think?"

"Wow, you people are snappy," he said. "I don't know. Let me see if I can find a way."

"Hurry," she said. She ran upstairs to my office and looked at Chris. "Dr. Johnson is going to try to find a way to find them."

"Good," he replied. "Now you're thinking."

Meanwhile in the warp zone, Heather and I were waiting to get a response from the tracking device. Then my watch rang. I looked at it and it read 5144. "Let's go," I said. We pushed the buttons on our belts. We programmed in 5144 and the Earth started to spin. Then we fell to the surface. "Be careful," I told Heather. "This is it." I knew our battle was coming closer. Then I heard thunder in the background and it started to rain. We ran out of the rain and under a building. It was dark and the sky was cloudy. Lightning was flashing across the sky and it was getting foggy. It was quiet and no one was around.

"Stay here," I said to Heather. "I am going to walk down the street." I started to walk away.

"Wait," she replied. "What if I get attacked?"

"I'll be right here," I said. Just as I said that I heard screeching. I looked and saw a flock of KATS flying toward us. Then the ground started to shake. "The battle is here," I said. "Get ready." Mountains appeared in front of us and then a platform grew from the ground and just floated from the ground. Lightning was striking everywhere. The KATS landed on the platform and then I saw Tyler and Jessy standing on the edge.

"How do we get up there," Heather asked. Just then a beam of light hit us and pulled us up. It was Tyler shooting some kind of transporting beam at us. When we got up there the KATS were screeching and waiting for the command to attack from Tyler. Tyler took out a gun and shot it at the air and a force field appeared. We could see Krissy and Chris through it.

"Chris," I screamed. "Krissy!!" I ran toward the water-like wall and touched it.

"They are looking for you but they are about to engage in a battle too," Tyler said. "And they will never get a chance to help you."

"You know that if they got here you wouldn't have a chance," Heather said. "You are afraid of the whole team together. Admit it Tyler; you wouldn't have a chance."

"Shut up," he said. "Are you that stupid? I am the most powerful force that ever walked the Earth."

"Well, we are about to destroy that force," I said. Tyler laughed.

"No chance," he replied. "You are too weak."

"That's what you think, but you are wrong," I answered. "We are the team that is about to destroy the most powerful force the world has ever seen. And we don't even need help from the KATS."

"We'll see about that," he said.

Meanwhile in the present, Dr. Johnson walked into Chris' office. "I found a way," he said.

"What is it," Chris asked.

"I don't need to tell you how to find them. I know where they are," he said.

"Where," Chris asked.

"The year 5144," he answered. Chris ran out of his office and told Krissy. Then they ran down to the basement and grabbed some equipment.

CHAPTER FOURTEEN

Chris and Krissy were getting ready to leave when they heard some explosions. They ran outside and looked around. The KATS were burning down buildings and destroying Washington, D.C. Then they saw Nick and Kelly standing on top of the Whitehouse. They shot a gun into the air and created a force field so Chris and Krissy could see us. "I think our battle takes place here," Chris said.

Meanwhile in the future, Heather and I looked at each other. I knew this was St. Louis because the mountain chains formed. Tyler expanded the force field so we could see Chris and Krissy more.

"Attack," Tyler said to the KATS. The KATS flew off the platform and started destroying the city.

"Let's get the KATS first," I said. We jumped off the platform and clicked our shoes together so we floated down to the ground. People were running around in chaos because the KATS were destroying everything. One of the KATS was going to attack a kid so I ran over and hit it in the back. It turned around and snarled at me. I picked up a metal pipe that was on the ground and hit it. It just shook its head.

"We need the crystals," Heather said.

"Go get them from us in the future," I said.

"I can't leave you," she replied.

"Go, I'll distract them." She hit her belt and disappeared. I kept fighting them with the pipe but it didn't even hurt them. A group of them came flying at me and I ran. I continued to try to stop the KATS. I realized I couldn't stop the KATS but I could stop their commanders.

I ran toward the platform and pulled out my long shot. I shot up to the platform. Jessy was waiting form me and kicked me in the face when I first got up there. I fell over. I got up and she punched me in the face and kicked me in the stomach. I got up and she threw me to the ground and stepped on my throat with her high heels. I grabbed her foot and pulled it forward and she fell backwards. I jumped up and she did too. She ran at me and I moved and she stopped just in enough time to miss falling off the edge. Tyler ran over and punched me in the face. Then he shot me with a bubble of time and it trapped me inside. It stung at my body with electricity. I started to punch at the bubble but I couldn't break it. Just then Heather appeared and shot it with her long shot. I fell to the ground and she threw a crystal at me. I caught it and smiled. Jessy ran at her and knocked her down. Tyler called the KATS to the platform. I held up the crystal and they all exploded. Tyler couldn't believe it. He was losing. He started to scream.

Meanwhile in the present, Nick and Kelly were enjoying the sight of the destruction that the KATS were committing. Chris and Krissy ran toward the Whitehouse

212

and used the long shot to shoot up to the top. They attacked Nick and Kelly. Chris punched Nick and he dropped the crystal. Kelly screamed for the KATS and they came flying over. Krissy grabbed the crystal that Nick dropped and held it up and the KATS exploded. Krissy then ran at Kelly and knocked her to the ground. She grabbed Kelly's crystal and threw it to Chris. Kelly and Nick stood up and disappeared.

Nick and Kelly reappeared on the platform by us. Chris and Krissy saw them appear by us through the force field. They hit there belts and appeared here also.

"No," Tyler yelled. "We have to keep them separated.

"Too late," I replied. "You are meeting your worst nightmare." Chris and Krissy ran over and met us.

"AHHH!!!!," Tyler was screaming. "Now I will lose."

"I Told you," I said. "Don't underestimate the power of our team." We lined up and so did his team. We clashed and battled.

CHAPTER FIFTEEN

Krissy and Kelly were fighting. Krissy ran at her and pushed her to the ground. Kelly got up and started hitting Krissy. The lightning was getting fierce and was striking the platform. Kelly hit Krissy and she fell to the ground. Lighting struck the ground and it started on fire. Tyler quickly used his power to guide the fire around the platform so there was no escape. Chris ran over and punched Kelly. Kelly slapped him and Nick grabbed Chris and threw him to the ground. Tyler was thinking of anything he could do to win. Kelly got up and pushed Krissy down to the ground. Krissy jumped up and knocked her over and started hitting Kelly in the face. The fire was heating the platform up. Tyler stood in the center of the platform and raised his arms into the air and the fire shot to the sky. He swung his arms around creating fireballs that were flying in all directions. We ducked and jumped to avoid them as much as we could. One hit Chris and lit him on fire. He dropped to the ground and started rolling around. I ran toward Tyler and knocked him down. When he hit the ground the fireballs disappeared. Chris put the fire out and stood up.

The city was on fire and being destroyed. Tyler lifted his arms and swung them and as he did balls of energy hit the city blowing the buildings to pieces. Krissy jumped up and kicked Kelly and she stumbled backwards and fell off the platform and into the burning city. Tyler started to scream and the storm intensified. Chris attacked Nick and knocked him to the ground. Tyler was still screaming and causing balls of energy to hit the city. Then when he knew it wasn't helping he pulled out his gun and shot it at Chris and Krissy. They disappeared into a black hole. He started to laugh. I ran toward Nick and knocked him backwards. He stumbled and almost fell of the platform but Tyler used wind to push him up. The rain was making the platform very slippery. Heather ran at Jessy and slid past her. She kept sliding toward the edge of the platform. She screamed for help and I ran over and grabbed her arm. We continued to slide. When we got to the edge I dug my feet into the ground and she hung over the side swinging. She looked down and saw the city on fire. Then she looked back up at me and I started to pull us up. When we got back up on the platform. Nick, Tyler and Jessy were standing in the middle.

"What were you saying about your team," he asked. He summoned more KATS. I pulled out the crystal but he shot it with his bubble gun and pulled it toward him. Heather pulled her crystal out but he did the same with hers. The KATS dove down at us and one picked Heather up and flew away. I looked at it as she was screaming for help. Tyler was laughing. Nick ran over to me and punched me. I punched him back and he stumbled backwards. He knocked me over and came running at me. I took my legs and flipped him over me and off the platform. Nick fell into the fiery pit. The KATS dropped Heather by Tyler and he handed her to Jessy. Jessy took her and tied her to stakes in the ground. Jessy stood by her and Tyler looked at me. He ran toward me and shot a bubble at me. He captured me and then shot a beam of electricity at the bubble. It knocked me unconscious and he tied me to the stakes too. He started to laugh.

"The world is mine," he screamed. "I win!!! I beat them. I am the Master of Time." The lightning intensified and it struck the ground near us. The flashes were so bright that I had to close my eyes. The wind was picking up and the thunder was getting louder. A tornado formed over the city. There was nothing we could do.

"Who doubted me," Tyler continued to scream. "They are wrong. The world is mine." Just then Chris and Krissy reappeared in back of him. Jessy saw them but Tyler was paying attention. She ran over to them and they threw her off the platform. Tyler turned around when he heard Jessy scream. He took the wind and blew Chris and Krissy off the platform but they hooked on with their hook shots. I wiggled loose from the stakes and stood up. Tyler was about to get rid of Chris and Krissy. I ran over and punched him in the back of the head. He turned around and hit me back. He pushed me toward the edge. We were right by the edge and we grabbed a hold of each other and I held on to him and jumped off. Heather screamed. I pulled out my long shot and shot it up to the platform. He grabbed onto my legs.

"Even if I die the war is not over," he told me with certainty.

"I'll take my chances," I told him. I shook my legs and he fell to the fiery city below. I pulled myself up to the platform. The storm stopped and the fire disappeared. I was breathing heavily and I walked over and helped Chris and Krissy up. Then we untied Heather. We beat him. The darkness disappeared. We warped back to the present day.

When we got back to the present day a mass of people were waiting for us and when they saw us they cheered. The president stood at the microphone and said "They beat the Master of Time. He is gone." The crowd cheered even louder. Some FBI agents walked over and shook our hands. They helped us through the crowd and to the president. Every station on TV was showing the unbelievable news and all around the world people were stunned that we had beat the Master of Time. People that were preparing for death were now jumping around and kissing the ground. "Thank you," the President said. "You have done your service. You are free to retire."

"Retire," I said. "Why would we retire?" I looked at the rest of the team and they laughed.

"The fun is just beginning," we said together. I walked over to the others.

"I learned today that we need to be a team," I said. "We will never succeed without each other."

"I agree," Heather said.

"What I'm saying," I continued, "is we need to decide if we are all in for life or if we are all out. But whatever it is, we have to do it together. And, not too surprisingly, I'm in."

"Me too," Heather said. "For you."

"Of course," Chris said.

"How could I say no," Krissy replied sarcastically. "You need me." We all laughed. I looked at Heather. I walked over and got down on my knees.

"Will you marry me," I asked. She looked at me in shock.

"Of course," she said as she got down on her knees in front of me. "I love you."
She hugged me and then gave me a kiss.

COMING NEXT IN THE SERIES

The team will take a relaxing camping trip. However, the trip ends in disaster and plagues the warriors' minds with a question. Why was Stonehenge built? The team will investigate that very question which will lead them to meet a scientist working in England. They'll soon discover that Stonehenge is a map of the sky built by an ancient civilization to track a universal force. That force is the Twelve Armies of the Zodiac. The team is going to have twelve days to defeat those twelve armies.

Two new members will join the team during the Zodiac mission. Those two new members will ask Krissy and Chris to explain how the team started. Then, while TJ and Heather are busy raising their newborn daughter, the new members will convince Chris and Krissy to take them back to paradise. The condition is that they are only there for ten minutes. However, a dino attack destroys the time belts and leaves them stranded in paradise. The problems is, no one knows that they left. TJ and Heather soon realize that something is wrong. They must face their fears to save their team.

A group following the Master of Time's beliefs will kidnap the leaders' daughter. The leaders will be led on a wild goose chase through time. This time, the group has a psychic with connections to some earthly elements to help. The rest of the team will have to master the four elements and then help the leaders' save their daughter and stop the group from taking over time.

DESTIFIRE ENTERTAINMENT PROJECTS

Time Warriors: Part Two Written by Tom Tancin and Chris Wolf

Time Warriors: Part Three Written by Tom Tancin and Chris Wolf

Time Warriors Part Four Written by Tom Tancin and Chris Wolf

Triton- Written By Tom Tancin. The story of the man who changed the Time Warriors. Relive his legacy.

Perfection- Written by Tom Tancin. When two geneticists decide to create the 'perfect' baby for themselves, they soon discover that what they created is the 'perfect' mistake.

Time Warriors A.C. Written by Tom Tancin and Chris Wolf After years of establishing themselves, and fighting to prove their innocence, the Time Warriors will become a true governmental agency. Time Warriors A.C. meets the team two years after the first series ended. Follow the team in the next set of missions.

FOR MORE INFORMATION PLEASE VISIT:

www.destifire.com

Acknowledgements

The basic idea of Atlantis, especially its landscape, was based on Plato's Timeaus and Critias. However, the story of Atlantis was adapted and modified from that of Plato's. The story of Atlantis and how it fell in this book is fiction created by the authors using Plato's account as a basis.

About the Authors

Tom Tancin was born on January 24, 1984. He lives in Northampton, PA with his parents and brother. He is currently a junior at Kutztown University of Pennsylvania studying biology/secondary education. He has a cat, two dogs, a bird, and a hamster. In his free time he enjoys writing, listening to music, and being with friends and family.

Chris Wolf was born on May 9, 1984. He lives in Danielsville, PA with his parents, grandmother, brother, and sister. He has a dog and two cats. He is currently one half of the creators of Time Warriors and Time Warriors A.C. and he also is the lead singer of a Christian rock band. He is very active in church.

Series Summary

When the United States creates a time machine after a close race with the other superpowers, they want to be the first to test it. The United States wants to make sure that they are the first to time travel, at any cost. Their targets become four young adults that will embark on the journey of a lifetime. However, that journey quickly becomes a nightmare.

The four young adults soon battle through time to save those who are innocent. They discover a group that is trying to take over society using the forces of time. The young adults become an agency to regulate time travel known as the Time Warriors. They are worshipped by the world as those who protect time. However, nothing ever goes smoothly.

It soon becomes apparent that there is more to their team than meets the eye. The truth is, their past was hidden from them, and they really don't know who they are. The world soon turns against them and a conspiracy shines through. The team soon realizes that they were setup from day one, and they embark on a quest to figure out who is responsible. The world of the warriors comes crashing down and they are forced to embark on the greatest challenge ever, proving their innocence. The team carries out twelve missions from the experiment to the final battle. In the process, they discover the secret of Atlantis, battle with the armies of the zodiac, visit a prehistoric paradise numerous times, battle with the Master of Time and his followers, take a field trip to ancient Egypt, and battle the four natural elements and the evil Karma. The final battle brings them face to face with Father Time.